To Win Her Heart

WITHIN THE CASTLE GATES BOOK TWO

CANDEE FICK

Contents

Prologue   1

Chapter One   7

Chapter Two   15

Chapter Three   23

Chapter Four   33

Chapter Five   45

Chapter Six   57

Chapter Seven   67

Chapter Eight   79

Chapter Nine   89

Chapter Ten   99

Chapter Eleven   109

Chapter Twelve   119

Chapter Thirteen   127

Preview: The Lost Heir   138

More Fiction   143

About Candee   145

Dedication

To all those who believe in fairy tales...
But don't feel like royalty.
This castle series is for you.

Become part of my family of readers and get a FREE novella plus access to exclusive bonus content. Sign up on my website at CandeeFick.com

Prologue

~March 1750; along the Cornwall coast

G rayson Wentworth dismounted from the hired carriage with stiff muscles and a sense of foreboding that left him as unstable as the earthquake-shaken ground had been near London four days before.

Over the long days journeying from Cambridge, his initial reluctance to leave his studies incomplete so close to graduation had been pushed aside by the exhilarating knowledge that, after nine years preparing to embrace his role as a future peer of the realm, he'd finally been summoned back to Wentworth Manor.

After stepping away from the panting horses and the coachman unloading his trunks, Grayson swiveled toward the arched openings in the high stone wall and inhaled the salty air thick with bittersweet memories and the stench of decaying fish rising from the seaside village of Danvers nestled among the rugged cliffs below.

No matter the reality awaiting inside, the familiar panoramic view from above the tiny harbor lifted his spirits. Even Cambridge with all the expected pomp of nobility and the weight of vaulted academia could not compete with the wild beauty of his birthplace.

There was no place he'd rather be.

If only his homecoming wasn't tainted by the report of his father's illness. The mere fact the Baron Danvers had admitted a weakness only heightened his trepidation.

Grayson turned toward the imposing yet regal structure perched like a castle above the commoners. But unlike the impressive buildings he'd left behind, this one wore a cloak of neglect. His gaze swept over the dingy window panes, faded whitewash, and dead foliage lingering around the foundation.

With winter's worst behind them, the necessary work should have at least been in progress by now. During his childhood, the Lenten season was spent preparing the heart to celebrate the resurrection…and preparing the manor house and surrounding fields for spring. In fact, along the road from Boscastle toward Danvers, both before and after the tin mine, he'd spied a number of plowed fields readied for planting.

Was the local delay a matter of money? Of time? Or the result of lazy servants without proper supervision?

A knot formed in his stomach. Something was definitely wrong and seemed to have been so for quite some time. Long before the brief letter bearing his father's seal had been dispatched to the university.

Grayson took a deep breath for courage before striding across the weed-infested cobblestones of the courtyard. Halfway up the leaf-littered exterior staircase, the front door burst open and a tardy footman bounded down the steps, proof that the household was in residence even if lax in their duties.

The errant employee paused a moment. "I'll fetch your baggage to your rooms, Master Grayson, er, sir."

Sir? Grayson flinched, then brushed aside his alarm. He wasn't a Sir anything…yet. With a quick nod at the young man, Grayson continued his way toward the entrance.

After crossing the threshold, he eyed the entryway with its mixture of polished woodwork and marble floor. The space was unchanged from his youth, including the sweeping staircase with the smooth banisters he'd attempted to slide down long before being shipped off to school.

That first memory sparked another of sneaking off to the kitchens for a snack between meals. In fact, his mouth already watered in anticipation of one of Mrs. Richard's treats.

Everything was as he'd remembered, except for the conspicuous absence of Mr. Munthorpe hovering about.

Over a week had passed since the message was sent, so would he find his father abed or in his study? Or dead? Despite the absence of black banners over the windows, the footman's formal greeting echoed ominously in his ears.

With quick steps, Grayson headed down the wide passage to the left of the main staircase, but stopped at a creaking noise overhead and retraced his steps.

"Master Grayson?"

Like the previous footman, their longtime head of staff had finally made an appearance.

"Munthorpe." Grayson met the silver-haired gentleman at the foot of the stairs. "At last, a familiar face to welcome me home." However, the years had taken their toll and it was hard to reconcile his memories with the gaunt and stooped man before him.

The man's smile widened as he inventoried the changes in Grayson's frame. After all, he'd left a boy and had returned a man. "The years have been good to you, lad." His smile faded. "You're needed above." Munthorpe pointed in the direction of the baron's bedchamber. "He did not wish to disturb your studies until it was absolutely necessary."

Grayson nodded, then headed up the grand staircase.

He'd been begging to come home for almost a decade, but had agreed to the last four years of advanced studies simply to keep his father happy. But no more. As a grown man, he'd fight to stay at the manor, a place where he was obviously needed.

At the top of the stairs, he glanced to his right toward the wing housing his childhood rooms and others for guests. Time enough to settle in later.

Grayson instead turned left toward his parents' suite and his late mother's private sitting room. The somewhat-threadbare rugs in the lavish hall muffled his steps, but the limited supply of candles reminded him again of the general sense of neglect he'd observed outside.

He needed to question Munthorpe and examine the books so he could get to work on a solution. But maintaining their property would have to wait because the estate's biggest problem lay down the hall.

Grayson paused at the entrance to the baron's bedroom. The door was ajar, but he knocked first out of habit. Not because after such a long absence, he felt like a stranger in his own home.

A cough, and then a weak voice. "Enter."

Grayson nudged his way into the darkened room where a fire blazed on the hearth.

"Welcome home, son." Lord Danvers's once forceful voice had been reduced to a mere whisper.

After swallowing the lump of emotion in his throat, Grayson quickly crossed to his father's side where he lay on the enormous mahogany four-posted bed. "I left the morning after your letter arrived. You should have sent for me sooner."

A frail hand lifted from the blankets to wave away his words.

The baron's faithful valet rose from a chair beside the bed and gestured for Grayson to take the seat.

"What happened?" Grayson's voice cracked and he fought to hide his horror at how his once robust sire had faded to a shriveled form buried beneath a mountain of blankets in the already sweltering room.

The valet glanced at his employer, then cleared his throat. "Months ago, my lord's new horse spooked and threw him to the ground, then trampled him. The physician said there were internal injuries in addition to his broken leg."

Grayson sank onto the padded chair as the faithful servant described the long journey through various infections and fevers. But just as his father seemed to be recovering, consumption had settled in his lungs. Despite his already-weakened condition and poor prognosis, the baron had still spent a fortune on doctors seeking a cure.

And since the estate's staff had been reduced as a result of their financial situation—and a previous small pox outbreak—there were now too many tasks spread among too few people.

"We need...your help. But...I'm sorry...to cut short...your education." His father's whispered apology ended in a violent coughing fit. The valet hurried to assist the baron into an upright position before propping more pillows behind him.

"I've learned enough." While the words were meant to soothe, they were also true. While meeting with his advising professor to explain his hasty departure, Grayson had learned that with the exception of one last academic paper that could be submitted via courier, the rest of his marks were sufficient to graduate at the end of the term. Besides, he'd never intended to actually sit for the bar like others of his classmates but rather to use his knowledge to benefit the region.

He would have been returning home in a few months regardless. And yet, all of those years at Cambridge had taken him away from his father's side. He'd been seated in a classroom or observing the inner workings of other estates instead of learning at his father's side and building ties with the local villagers.

Finally done coughing, the baron collapsed back against the pillows and wiped a handkerchief across his lips. The white linen came away stained with bloody phlegm.

Grayson's heart clenched. All those years he could have spent with his sole remaining family member instead of arriving home to bury his father.

There would be no new life this Easter season, only another grave. And only God to comfort him.

Until the inevitable happened, however, he vowed to ease his father's suffering and make every moment count.

The normally stern visage of the baron had melted into that of a broken man. "Take care...of the place...your mother...loved it so."

Swallowing the lump in his throat at the childhood memories of his mother, Grayson gently squeezed his father's hand. "I will."

"Won't be here...to guide you." Another whisper, followed by a frown.

As if he worried his son would not be able to run the estate without guidance.

As if his heir was unfit.

Grayson again fought the urge to retreat to the study to examine their accounts before touring the estate. Once armed with information, he could better ease his father's worries. And yet, his years of education were not in vain. "I know what to do. Between my boyhood memories and Cambridge, I'm prepared. And if I have any questions, I can always ask Munthorpe. In the meantime, you need to rest."

The exhausted lord nodded, then relaxed deeper into the pillows. "One more...thing...and I...can be...at peace."

Based on the blueish-gray cast to his father's skin, the end was near. In a sudden rush of emotion, all Grayson's past hurts were replaced by the keen desire to please his father one more time.

"Anything."

"Promise...me." The ghost of a smile flitted across his father's gaunt face. "Find a wife."

At Cambridge, he'd suffered numerous encounters with matchmaking mothers and their vapid daughters, making a wife the last thing on his mind. And yet, he would need to marry eventually to produce an heir and continue the Wentworth line.

"I will." Agreement came easily since it bore no timetable.

"Find a wife...and win her heart."

A neglected longing stirred within.

Maybe someday this cold home would once again ring with laughter and music like when his mother had lived.

Chapter One

June 1750, Whitstone, Cornwall

H ow many different shades of blue were there?

Emma Richards stretched her sample of thread across the assortment of spools on display in the Whitstone village warehouse and wished for better light.

"Find what you need yet, Miss Emma?"

She glanced up from her frustrating search to find Mrs. Talbot clutching a paper-wrapped package to her ample bosom. "Somewhat." Emma waved a hand at the red and yellow strands her older cousins had requested for their latest embroidery project. "But I'm still having trouble finding thread to match the fabric of Phoebe's dress."

The shopkeeper's wife set her package on the wooden counter and leaned closer. "Shouldn't the dressmaker be charged with that task?" She poked a stout finger at the spools with a frown. "It would be easier if you'd brought a sample of the fabric instead of a single thread."

Emma sighed. "She demanded that the upstairs maid repair the torn hem today but refused to let the gown out of her room. This thread was pulled from the inside of a seam and will have to do."

"And of course you were sent on the errand."

"I volunteered." Anything to get out of the house for a few hours, especially in the middle of the week.

The other woman grunted, then squinted at the thread. "Let me take a closer look."

Emma gripped the precious bit of silk between two fingers and held it up to the light streaming in the dusty window. "The shade is somewhere between the blue of a summer sky after a rain and that of a robin's egg in its nest. She says it matches her eyes."

"Sounds like something from a poem in a book like the one Miss Julia ordered." Mrs. Talbot tapped the mystery package, then held two different spools up to the light. "If you're to err, err on the lighter side. But it shouldn't be too noticeable along the hem anyway."

"Especially in the back." However, with Phoebe's temperament, one never knew. But she didn't have time to dawdle. Emma picked the lighter shade and added it to the pile of her other purchases.

"Anything else you need?"

"Our cook asked for more cloves and some saffron if you have any."

"Another fancy dinner party tonight?"

Emma smiled. "Why else would repairing a favorite gown be so important?"

While the shopkeeper's wife busied herself measuring the spices into small muslin drawstring bags, the door opened and Mrs. Pratt entered followed by Mrs. Pembroke. As the newcomers approached their friend, Emma sidestepped into the shadows under the pretense of examining the dress goods.

After all, when the trio got together, gossip spread faster than the wind blew and she had no desire to be dragged into their dramatics.

"You'll never guess who's staying at the inn tonight. Such important guests on a Wednesday, no less."

"Oh?" Mrs. Talbot cast a glance at Emma. "But are they dining with you or with the baron?"

Mrs. Pratt grunted as if her choicest tidbit of information had been stolen. "Well, at the manor. But that can only suggest a wedding is on the horizon." She elbowed the vicar's wife. "Have you heard anything?"

"Not specifically. However..." Mrs. Pembroke glanced around the cluttered shop, frowned at Emma, then lowered her voice to a mere whisper.

As if Emma cared about the evening's specific guest list or even the identity of the last minute addition. One snooty nobleman was much like the others who paraded through the manor's ornate dining room in pursuit of her cousins. Except the only guests worse than the idle rich were her uncle's lecherous friends and business associates.

Not that it mattered because she wouldn't be present to find out.

"In her note, the countess Wexley specifically asked if I had access to fresh strawberries to serve with their breakfast."

"My Joffrey brought in a few this morning if you want to check them over." Mrs. Talbot hoisted a wooden box onto the end of the counter and Mrs. Pratt's eyes lit up.

"Those will be perfect. I'll take the whole box."

The sight of the juicy berries set Emma's mouth to watering and she could almost taste her mother's pastries. The memory stirred a bittersweet longing for home.

Emma cleared the emotion from her throat, then stepped forward. "Could you please add three measures of your finest ground flour to my order as well? I would hate for us to run out with guests." Especially since she hoped to do a little private baking on the morrow.

"Certainly miss." Mrs. Talbot turned to scoop flour from a barrel into a larger muslin sack.

Mrs. Pembroke jostled her way to Emma's side. "What do you hear about Midsummer's Eve? Is the baron going to host a larger celebration this year or not?"

"I'm not privy to any specific plans as of yet." As if the baron or his sister would tell her anything.

The trio of village gossips filled in the gaps of her non-answer with plenty of speculation and wishful thinking.

A few minutes later, with her purchases recorded in the shop's ledger under the manor's account, Emma collected the assortment of packages into her basket and bid the women farewell.

Once outside the stone building, she took the road out of the village at a brisk pace. Breathing deep, she tilted her chin up to soak in the rare sunshine during her walk.

June had always been her favorite time of year.

Between the longer days and the lush green of the surrounding fields with their emerging crops, like the village women, she already counted down until Midsummer's Eve. Even if the local celebration paled in the shadow of her childhood memories, at least it was something to look forward to.

Then again, nothing could live up to majestic views from her former home on the Cornwall coast just miles from the castle of Tintagel and the legendary birthplace of King Arthur. Of course, her mother had done her best to make the stories of the historic ruler and his faithful knights ride through her dreams at night. And growing up under the shadow of a different castle on the hill, only fueled her imagination.

With a sigh, Emma shifted her heavy basket from one arm to the other and continued down the dusty road toward Bainbridge Manor. A few paces ahead, the road curved to run along the edge of the tributary feeding into the River Neet and her greedy ears strained for the sound of trickling over the smooth stones of the creek bed as the water rushed onward to feed the sea.

It was the closest she'd come to the crashing waves of her home—make that former home—in over two years.

Emma swallowed the bitter ache of her grief. Losing her parents had been one thing, but being uprooted from the only community she'd ever known had been a difficult transition.

Especially since everything around Whitstone was so flat, unlike the cliffs of the rugged coast. Not to mention they were far enough inland that she couldn't even catch a whiff of the sea.

Instead the scent of moist earth and the hedging plants would have been a vast improvement over the pungent aroma of cattle and sheep dung wafting from the farmland to the north of the manor.

Before long, the road took a sharp bend to the right, transforming into a rugged stone arch that spanned the river.

After a few restorative minutes dawdling near the middle of the bridge and soaking up the sounds of rushing water to inspire her dreams, Emma continued her trek. Soon she turned off the main road onto the lane leading to her current home.

If one could call the ostentatious three-storied structure a home even if her father had been raised there before joining the military and going off to sea.

Lord Bainbridge, her uncle by blood, had expanded the Tudor era buildings of Bainbridge Manor and even erected decorative scrolled iron gates to guard the entrance to his virtual kingdom. Meanwhile, his sister—Lady Rowley—had filled the rooms with luxurious treasures brought from all over the world.

The cumulative effect seemed more than a little pretentious as if the baron aimed to appear more important than he truly was. Then again, with the number of guests they'd entertained over the past year since the household's official mourning period had ended, her uncle's ambition had paid off with connections far and wide. Connections that only served to boost his powerful hold over the local trade routes and if rumors were true, added even more coin to his coffers.

Coins she would never see.

At last, Emma reached the cobblestoned circle drive leading to the grand entrance to the manor house, then turned down the gravel path between the coach house and the main building. Ahead lay the servant's entrance.

A virtual fist closed around her heart and Emma fingered her mother's tin locket resting above the square neckline of her faded green gown. The memory of her mother's love did as much to ease her pain as Emma's clinging to the vicar's private words that God was a father to the fatherless.

The other Clarkes and Lady Rowley could have been her family instead of simply housing their destitute orphaned relative. Two years ago she'd been settled into a room at the end of the family's wing, not to solidify the family bond but only to ensure a quick response to their summons.

Their gift of a roof over her head came with strings. Emma now found herself in the awkward position of a glorified servant who could not be fired...but did not receive wages either. An errand girl and convenient companion for her cousins. And a woman whose lack of a definitive role within the hierarchy of household staff distanced her from any companionship belowstairs.

Without true friends and ever aware of the curious glances, she spent her days trying to be helpful wherever she could and then escaped to her small bedchamber to dream of King Arthur and a castle by the sea.

With a deep breath for patience, Emma pushed open the door and stepped into the large kitchen. As her eyes adjusted to the dimmer light, she caught snippets of conversation between two kitchen maids busy chopping vegetables and churning butter.

Apparently while she'd been at the village, one of the upstairs maids had been fired and with many of the other staff members already assigned to accompany the ladies of the house during their various activities and the day's outings, the third kitchen maid had been required to fill the housekeeping gap abovestairs.

With three marriageable maidens under one roof, the staff was already sometimes stretched thin. But with additional guests coming for dinner, today was the worst possible day for them to be left shorthanded.

Perhaps today was the day she could finally prove useful.

A smile tugged at Emma's lips as she approached Mrs. Ashbrook near the open fire. "I obtained the spices you asked for as well as an extra supply of fine flour for pastries."

The main cook nodded as she turned the slabs of meat roasting over the flames. "Thank you, dear. Except I don't see as how we'll have time for much baking today. I'm already behind and still need to check the place settings."

"Oh, I can do that for you. And my mother loved to bake so I would be happy to mix the dough, too." Emma held her breath as the older woman frowned.

"If'n you don't mind, I wouldn't have to adjust the menu for tonight after all. Could you make more bread and some sort of dessert?"

"Of course." Emma's smile broke free. "Perhaps I could fix something with strawberries. I happened to overhear in the village that Lady Wexley has been asking for them."

Mrs. Ashbrook's eyes lit up and she raised her voice. "Caroline, once you've put the butter in the molds, I need you to pick a large bowl of strawberries."

Across the room, the other girl grumbled, but Emma ignored her complaints, instead heading into the pantry to put the new spices away. After setting her basket with her cousins' thread and book near the servants' stairs to deliver later, Emma put on an apron and gathered the ingredients she needed.

The familiar motions of mixing and kneading the dough brought back precious memories of learning to bake beside her mother. Back when life was simpler even if they were poor.

Back when her days were spent creating lovely things from simple ingredients.

Perhaps, God willing, someday she could find a way to make that precious memory a reality again. But for now, it was her responsibility to help the true daughters of the household make good matches. Starting with entertaining all of their guests that evening.

Once the bread dough was set to rise, she'd head to the dining room to check the table linens.

Chapter Two

G rayson dug his heels into his horse's flanks, nudging the beast along the road from Boscastle's harbor inland toward the heart of Cornwall.

The rare sunshine did little to boost his mood because God alone knew the outcome of his mission and if it would bode well for the future of Danvers. Or not.

Within days of burying his sire and assuming the title, Grayson had processed his grief by devoting his attention to the manor's accounts and tending to the surrounding estate. Then while digging through the recesses of his father's desk, he had unearthed additional stacks of paperwork detailing even more unfinished business.

Two months later, the burden of his additional responsibilities still weighed upon his shoulders.

God only knew if he was capable of leading his people in a way that would bring honor to the Wentworth name. Or if he would be the last of a line dating back to the days of King Henry VIII.

Now only two tasks remained...and one of them could provide Danvers financial stability at the cost of his heart. Was it too steep a price to pay?

Since there was only one way to know for sure, Grayson pushed his mount into a slow gallop. Fifteen minutes later, as he neared the intersection with the main trade route through the region, he caught up with a slow-moving wagon laden with barrels and crates.

A wagon guarded by a trio of fierce looking men armed with pistols instead of the expected farmer or his son.

The hair on the back of his neck stood on end, but without adequate protection of his own, he dared not ask their business. Although, if smugglers felt confident enough to transport goods in broad daylight, it appeared the local magistrate had turned a blind eye to their activity. Perhaps in exchange for a piece of the profits.

While his stomach churned at the ethical dilemma of ignoring the illegal activities that defied the unpopular orders of King George II but provided a livelihood for his people, Grayson spurred his horse on and turned east onto the larger thoroughfare toward his destination. After all, he had his own future to secure first.

If only his father had paid more attention to his affairs before his final illness.

After another hour of cantering, he finally arrived at the village of Whitstone and stopped a passing boy for directions to the inn. Minutes later, he dismounted in front of the modest two-story building. After releasing his baggage from behind the saddle, he handed the care of his horse over to a stable boy and strode toward the door.

Once inside, he removed his hat and glanced around as his eyes adjusted to the dim lighting.

"Good noon." A balding man with a significant paunch rose from one of the benches flanking a row of half-occupied tables and sauntered across the room.

"Good noon yourself." Grayson dropped his bags onto the floor near the wall and dusted off his hands. "I am Grayson...Sir Grayson Wentworth."

The man's graying eyebrows rose at his bumbling introduction. "Lord Danvers?"

Other conversations in the room suddenly stopped and multiple eyes swiveled his direction. Likely the whole region had heard of his father's passing by now and was eager for a look at his heir.

Grayson resisted the urge to squirm under the attention. "Aye. I sent word—"

Whatever else he'd wanted to say was interrupted by the arrival of a middle-aged thin woman with sharp eyes and a large box of strawberries. "Charles?" The newcomer shoved her burden into the arms of the man, then pushed him toward the kitchen. "Put those somewhere safe and don't you dare touch them. They're for the countess."

"Countess? How many rooms does your inn have?" Grayson eyed the ceiling trying to imagine the layout overhead.

"Who are you?" The woman's critical gaze narrowed at the road dust that had settled on his fitted jacket, breeches, and riding boots.

"Mary, mind your manners. This be the new Lord Danvers." The innkeeper shrugged. "While I'm playing errand boy and me wife, Mrs. Pratt, explains the rest, can I fetch you something to eat?"

Grayson nodded. He'd been away from Cornwall too long if this was the typical reception for a peer of the realm. Although, if they were already fetching berries for a countess...

"My apologies, Lord Danvers." The woman bobbed a stiff curtsy. "The Earl of Wexley, his lady, and their son the viscount Egerton sent word this morning of their impending arrival so while we can offer ye a fine meal, there are no longer any rooms available."

Outranked and ousted to boot.

Now where was he supposed to sleep? Because it wouldn't do at all to impose upon the local baron's hospitality unless invited.

"Now don't you worry none, m'lord. I'll send a lad over to the vicar's. The vicarage is right off the road on the far side of town and the Reverend and Mrs. Pembroke would be glad to offer their hospitality for as long as you'll be in the area."

The last bit was spoken like a question, but before he could form a diplomatic deflection, the innkeeper was back with a simple luncheon.

An hour later, he was subjected to another awkward introduction to his new—and hopefully temporary—hosts while being visually evaluated by the vicar's beady-eyed wife.

Mrs. Pratt and Mrs. Pembroke were two of a kind. That birds of a feather comparison was on full display as the woman showed him to a simple room.

"I'll bring you a fresh ewer of water if you wish to wash up before you..." The woman could have been a fisherwife the way she dangled her hook hoping he would take the bait and reveal either his destination or his purpose.

He bit his lip to hide a smile. "Please do. My ride today seems to have stirred up a fair share of dust."

Her shoulders slumped at his non-answer to her real question, but even though she turned to fetch the water, she paused in the doorway. "If I might ask, why just a horse and not a carriage like others of your rank?"

"Do you have many carriages pass through this village?"

"A few. And the blacksmith keeps one for hire behind the livery." She shook her head and offered a wry glance over her shoulder. "You're a wily one, m'lord."

"So my mother always said." His low chuckle followed her out of the room.

All it had taken was a little verbal sparring to bring the first smile to his face in months. Perhaps it was a good omen for a favorable outcome to the day's business.

Taking advantage of his limited time before the meddling interrogation resumed, Grayson unpacked his clothing and hung it in the wardrobe. The truth was, he did not know how long he would be in the area and had only brought the minimum of what he might need. And it was cheaper to board a single horse than store an unused carriage, feed a team of horses, and house his coachman especially when his limited resources were best used elsewhere.

God, please go before me to prepare the way.

The knot in his midsection tightened. Perhaps it would be better to get an early start and conduct his business before the dinner hour.

After a quick wash, he changed into fresh clothes, folded his dinner jacket into a small satchel with his papers, and sought out the vicar to get directions to the manor. Not that the man was likely to keep a secret from his wife but at least he could celebrate the fact she hadn't gotten the information from him.

It was a small victory, but one he savored for the time it took to saddle his horse and head down the road again.

Not far beyond the outskirts of the village, he caught the sound of feminine laughter to his right. On the far side of the gently flowing river across a wooden footbridge, a young woman in a pink gown strolled arm-in-arm with a fastidiously-attired man with obviously enough means to dress in the latest fashion of the royal court.

When the woman rested her blonde head against her companion's shoulder, it was obvious that the couple were in love. And based on the presence of the liveried footman overseeing the remnants of a picnic spread out upon a blanket, they were yet in the courtship stage of their relationship.

A curious process he'd observed multiple times with other couples he'd spied upon while growing up in Danvers. Not to mention even similar scenes here and there around Cambridge.

If only he was free to find his own wife.

He'd thought he had plenty of time to honor his promise to his dying father, but while sorting through his father's papers, he'd come across the letter that changed everything.

The letter that set him on this road of duty instead of one of his choosing.

Grayson reined his mount back to a slow walk to match the cumbersome dread in his stomach. Because the heavy burden upon his shoulders was more than grief or the assuming of his father's title as baron and guardian to several children orphaned in the last small pox outbreak, but rather a lifetime commitment to a family obligation.

He'd give anything to be back at Wentworth Manor above Danvers, but only a few tasks remained including tracking down the last heir named in his father's will. Not to mention, his vow to his father must be upheld. Wentworths never broke their word.

After following the road around the bend and across the stone bridge, Grayson turned off on the lane the vicar had described and eventually came to the ornate gates marking the entrance to the lavish estate and the massive house beyond.

His father's associate, the Baron Bainbridge, had obviously done well for himself and risen far above his ancestor's position as a merchant situated along the main inland trade routes. And knowing that a former king had handed out titles to baronies in exchange for financial contributions, the power-grabbing situation was even clearer.

If only the memory of an overly-laden and well-guarded wagon had not chosen that moment to intrude.

Grayson spurred his horse along the circular drive and approached the grand entrance to the baron's home where a stable boy rushed forward to lead his horse away.

Leaving Grayson alone beside the wide stairs leading up to the ornately carved front entrance. An entrance that typically would have already been held open by a footman.

After a moment's pause for courage, Grayson climbed the stairs and opened the door himself. Once inside, he noted the expensively appointed entryway, but despite sending a note earlier in the week to announce his intentions to visit and the subsequent invitation to dinner, the lack of welcome was disconcerting.

He shook off the painful comparison to his recent homecoming and squared his shoulders. "Hallo? Anyone here?"

A loud gasp came from somewhere to his right and he took a few steps that direction to investigate.

A young woman emerged from the dining room with an armload of table linens clutched against the apron covering her simple dress. He caught a glimpse of her green eyes flitting over his attire before she averted her gaze and curtsied as befitting her position.

And his.

It was a reaction he had yet to adjust to without the familiar twinge of grief.

Grayson cleared his throat. "I'm here to see Lord Bainbridge. I know he's expecting me for dinner this evening, but I had good weather for travel and arrived early. Perhaps he is available to discuss our business this afternoon?"

"My apologies for the absence of our head of staff to assist you, but he was called away by other duties. We are a bit short-handed at the moment." Her soft voice held a mixture of Cornwall and culture. "I believe his lordship is currently out overseeing his properties with his steward."

Disappointment swirled with relief at having his meeting delayed. And yet, what would he do with himself while he waited?

"You're welcome to wait in the library across the hall where I can bring you a tea tray. Or I can show you to a guest room first if you prefer to freshen up after your journey."

The maid's comments only served to remind him of the dust on his boots and the fact he'd arrived unfashionably early.

His face heated. He'd been a fool to neglect the protocol of the classes, but as much as he wanted to bluster his way through the breech of etiquette while adjusting to his new title, he wished for a moment of normalcy.

A moment to simply be a man instead of a baron.

Perhaps he could propose a compromise to benefit them both?

"If you are so short-handed, I'd hate for my early arrival to set you further behind in your duties." He waved a hand at the folded cloth in her arms, wishing for another glimpse of her eyes rather than the top of her chestnut-colored hair. "Perhaps you could show me to the kitchens where I could get a snack to tide me over?"

With another gasp, she finally lifted her horrified gaze to his. "It wouldn't be proper."

"Doesn't the guest always get what he wants?"

A flash of something in her intriguing eyes reminded him of the swirling green of the storm-tossed sea along the cliffs near home. As if his question offended her somehow.

He held up a placating hand. "All I'm asking for is a bite to eat somewhere other than a stuffy library. Surely being around a little conversation is better than stacks of dusty books."

She sighed and a smile flickered around her lips. "As you wish, m'lord. Give me a moment to finish sorting these linens and I will lead you back."

Grayson nodded, then followed her to the dining room where she scurried around the intimidatingly large table. A table where he'd be dining in a few hours and once again feeling out of his element. Followed by an uncomfortable conversation where he could only hope to conduct his business without losing the man's respect.

But at least for the time being, he could push aside his somewhat unwelcome position for a few more minutes.

Chapter Three

E mma's wide skirts swayed around her ankles but did nothing to distract her from the uncomfortable awareness of the young lord following her down the servant's hallway. The steady tread of his boots on the boards behind her did nothing to slow her pulse either.

Well, in all fairness, it wasn't every day that a handsome man gave her his full attention. If only she could forget the way the cut of his jacket hugged his broad shoulders or the rich color of his unpowdered hair swept back off his forehead before being tied at his nape with a black ribbon.

She pressed a hand against the flutter of attraction in her belly, then pushed through the doorway into the kitchen.

"Is everything..." Mrs. Ashbrook's voice trailed off as she spied the man behind Emma.

"The dining room is well in hand, but this gentleman—"

"Demanded that his cup of tea be served around people instead of alone with only books to keep him company." The baron's guest stopped beside her and his deep voice triggered an answering warmth in her chest. "If you please. I have fond memories of spending time in the kitchens when I was a boy."

Mrs. Ashbrook laid her large stirring spoon beside the nearest pot and reached for the kettle instead. "You are welcome. Pull up a stool over here and make yourself comfortable, but take care lest we put you to work."

Across the room, the lone remaining kitchen maid giggled.

"Speaking of idle hands..." The cook speared a glance at the far worktable. "You should be done with your chopping by now. Go help Caroline pick the rest of the produce then I have more tasks for the two of you."

"Yes, ma'am." Hannah sighed, then disappeared through the outer door toward the gardens.

"I'll pour his tea while you see to the rest of a tray for our guest." Mrs. Ashbrook tilted her head toward the pantry.

"Do not go to much trouble on my account." The intruder removed his coat and hung it on a wall hook along with a leather satchel before crossing over to the designated stool. "I am more content with bread and cheese than finger sandwiches." He pushed up the plain cuffs on his white shirt-sleeves revealing muscular forearms, tanned as if he'd been working out-of-doors lately.

Emma gulped at the sight, then with a burning face, escaped to the storage rooms where she collected a chunk of cheddar cheese and a small loaf of wheat bread onto a tray along with a paring knife.

She paused before returning to the warm kitchen. Why did he have to seem more like a normal man than a wealthy guest or a usual visitor for the baron? But since he appeared to be in his early twenties, he was probably yet another suitor for one of her cousins.

Who would be the lucky bride?

She took a deep breath and pasted a serene smile on her face, then stepped into the room to deliver the simple tray. After setting the wooden platter near his elbow, she moved toward the mound of bread dough but was stopped by a warm hand on her elbow that quickly disappeared.

"Thank you, miss."

She darted a quick glance his direction and was captured by his grayish-blue eyes. A unique shade that triggered a flash of recognition that quickly faded. After all, those same eyes that now radiated kindness had earlier held a teasing glint when he'd begged his way into the kitchens instead of the library.

Something about the mixture of compassion and mischief seemed familiar, but it was much too late to ask his name. Nor would it be proper to continue staring until something triggered her wayward memory.

Instead, she nodded an acknowledgment, then rounded the waist-high worktable to turn out the batch of dough onto the floured surface.

With shaking hands, she sprinkled additional flour atop the sticky mass, then risked another glance across the tabletop at the mysterious nobleman nibbling away at his light meal and chatting with the cook about the weather.

Even in his shirtsleeves, he was obviously a prize on the marriage market. And she was not worthy of consideration. Without a dowry...and with little hope of one from her uncle especially after her aunt's passing and his ultimatum, her foolish childhood dreams would go unfulfilled.

No knight from any table—round or otherwise—would be coming to her rescue. At best she was destined to a lifetime kneading bread in someone else's kitchen.

Taking out her frustrations on the unwieldy dough, she gradually began to relax. Especially with her hands occupied in the familiar task of shaping the loaves under the approving eye of the friendly cook.

With the hint of a smile, Mrs. Ashbrook drew Emma into the conversation with a debate about the merits of venison over mutton.

They had just moved on to the question of whether bread pudding was too humble of a dish to be served in faraway London, when Hannah and Caroline returned with a giant bowl of berries and two baskets of other vegetables.

Immediately, one was sent back outdoors to shell the peas and the other to the butler's station to polish the silver. Almost as if Mrs. Ashbrook wanted to keep the young lord away from the girls. Or them away from him.

Emma glanced at the cook in time to catch a quick wink in her direction and she fought a grin at the realization she had a matchmaking ally within the walls of the manor.

Once again, heat bloomed on her face and Emma covered her nerves by transferring the unbaked loaves into the oven. With that task done, she quickly cleaned her station and began mixing a batch of the pastry dough instead.

"What are you making now?" Their noble visitor pushed aside his emptied dishes.

"I planned to fill pockets of pastry dough with pureed fruit and dust them with sugar."

His eyes shifted toward a deeper blue tint. "When I was growing up, our cook made something similar. She has since passed away and I had almost forgotten."

Emma blinked back tears at the memory of learning this recipe at her mother's side. "What was your favorite filling?" Perhaps she could make a second batch especially for him.

What was she thinking? No. While it was good to keep their guests happy, it wouldn't do to get to invested in their lives.

"Hmm." He tapped a long finger against his lips. "In the fall, apple slices with cinnamon were my favorite. But anything with berries was a close second. I missed those while away at school."

"School?" At the insistence of her mother because of her heritage, the village vicar had taught her to read and write unlike most girls along the coast, but she knew that boys from the upper class were often sent away from home.

"Ah, yes. I was gone for years, most recently at Cambridge." A hint of something in his tone tugged at her heart. "I've been too busy since returning home to search our gardens for a neglected berry patch."

The desire to cheer him rose up within. "Well, you're in luck. Caroline just picked a bowl of strawberries." She tilted her head toward the far counter where the unattended bowl waited for her attention.

A laugh burst from his lips. "There were strawberries at the inn, too. I can't seem to escape them, but I have to admit I'm eager for a taste."

Her heart stuttered. The inn? Of course Mrs. Pratt had bought a box for her guest the countess. Did that mean this man was already married or was he traveling with his mother? If so, he was even further from her league than she'd thought. But then why would he desire to spend time in the kitchens of a stranger's home?

"If I can't have some here, I'll have to ask the vicar's wife if she can point out a patch instead."

Emma's heart relaxed to know he was staying at the vicarage and a smile bloomed on her face again.

Mrs. Ashbrook just shook her head, then picked up an empty basket and disappeared out the door toward the gardens. Leaving them alone and mostly unchaperoned.

"If you want to clean the berries for this batch, I'll make a second batch with dried apples and cinnamon just for you." Emma blinked as the unexpected offer crossed her lips. And yet, it was equally surprising how comfortable she felt around their mysterious guest.

"You would?"

"I would. But I'd need help so I don't fall behind in my duties." She tilted her head toward the bowl and fought to contain her grin.

"It would be my pleasure, especially since I'd reap the rewards." He stood and crossed the kitchen.

A half hour later, Grayson snatched a slice of dried apple from the bowl of water where it had been soaking and popped it into his mouth.

Almost before he had a chance to chew, a hand slapped his arm. "Don't you be—" The young woman beside him gasped, then tried to brush the flour from his sleeve. "I'm so sorry, m'lord. I forgot myself."

"Forgot what?"

"That you're a...And I'm a..." She sputtered to a stop then took a deep breath. "I don't know of any nobility who would be caught getting their hands dirty in the kitchens."

"True." A smile curved his lips. "It seems I've forgotten myself for a bit too." And that was a good thing to remember he could still be his own man despite the new title and weight of responsibilities. "This has been exactly the distraction I've needed. But I'm here to see this task through, so since I'm done mashing the berries and mixing in the honey, what's next?"

She dropped a ball of dough onto the table and picked up a rolling pin. "We'll leave the apples *alone* to soak awhile longer and start assembling the other pastries first."

"If you insist." He moved the apples out of the way and watched as she rolled the dough out flat, then reached for a knife to quickly slice it into wide rows.

"Now you can spoon the berries into the center of each square." Another swipe of the knife and the promised squares began to emerge.

"How much for each?" Grayson nestled the bowl in the crook of his arm and scooped a large dollop onto the closest spot. "Like that?"

"Maybe just a bit less so we have room to seal the dough around the filling." She paused her cutting to fold the first square in half diagonally, creating a triangular pocket. "I sometimes use a little water on my fingertip to moisten the seam, but then we'll use a fork to score the final edges."

Just like the ones Mrs. Richards used to make when he was a boy. Back when he used to sneak into the kitchen for her warm mothering touch. Too bad it seemed his favorite treat was a common recipe after all.

He continued to spoon out the filling while the pretty baker finished her slicing, then moved to his other side to start folding the dough.

If only he knew her name.

Because despite the simple green gown beneath her apron and her chestnut-colored hair pulled back into a tidy bun at the nape of her neck, her friendly smile and competence in the kitchen tugged even more of his happy childhood memories to the surface.

After dividing the last of the berries onto the dough, he set the empty bowl aside and attempted to fold his first pocket. Except it wouldn't stick together. Right. A dab of water stolen from the bowl of apples.

Followed by a snicker beside him.

He grinned in response. He hadn't had this much fun in years.

As he worked his way down the row toward her, he caught her sideways glance at him. As if she tried to figure him out but not in a bad way. Almost as if she respected him more for his willingness to get his hands dirty. And maybe even his kind treatment of the staff.

Including the friendly cook who seemed to have disappeared along with the other kitchen help.

"Emma? Where are you?" A strident voice echoed down the hall from the direction of the dining room and the main entry.

Beside him, the baker stiffened but continued her work, beginning to transfer the assembled pastries from the table to a thin metal sheet.

"Aha. There you are." A young woman appeared in the doorway, the large hooped skirt of her pink gown swaying at her sudden stop.

Grayson realized several things at once.

First, the lovely baker's name was Emma. And second, he'd seen the newcomer earlier along the river with her beau. He sneaked another glance at the rosy-cheeked beauty—likely one of the baron's daughters—taking in the elaborately curled hair gathered at the top of her head, her blue eyes, and the fact she was younger than he'd originally thought.

An instant later, her nose wrinkled and she sniffed in disgust at the sight of them with sticky dough on their fingers and shifted her gaze above their heads. "Papa already said you're to help me with whatever I need, so I don't know why I need to track you down every time after I go out."

Hmm. So the kitchen helper was actually a ladies maid? Were they short on funds for adequate help? Or merely shorthanded like...Emma...had said earlier?

"My apologies, Phoebe, but I did not know when you might return. And in the meantime, I was also needed to help here. What can I do for you?" Emma's words were respectfully appropriate, but held an undertone of strained patience as if this was a familiar exchange.

"I need a bath and tea brought up to my room so I can get ready for tonight." The young Miss Clarke propped her hands on her hips. "And did you find any thread to match? Because my gown still needs mending, then pressing. Molly's incompetent and the last time she left a crease along the hem."

The hem? As if anyone would notice.

Grayson pressed down hard on the seam of yet another fruit-filled pocket remembering a certain folded paper in his satchel. Hopefully the other daughters in the household weren't as spoiled.

Then again, he was grateful for the glimpse into the truth of the girl's attitude without the proper societal facade he would likely see at dinner.

Emma murmured something about Molly not being around to touch the dress, then began to mix ingredients for another batch of dough as she had promised.

But Miss Phoebe wasn't done.

"I can't believe Papa added that stuffy old baron to the guest list for dinner."

Grayson swallowed his laughter at the description that might have fit his father, but certainly didn't fit him. Unless there was yet another baron arriving soon.

Suddenly he wished he hadn't followed his lonely heart back to the kitchens. At least not without properly introducing himself first. Then again, there was only one way to remedy the situation now.

He straightened. "About that—"

The beauty cut him off with a frown and a pointed glance at his dirty hands. "I invited Francis, Mr. Smythe, as my dinner partner and I have to look my best. He has asked me to marry him and I have agreed, so now all I have to do is convince Papa to accept his suit." The young lady of the house twirled a curl around one finger of her lily-white hand.

A hand that had never done a hard day's work. Hands like his mother's. Unlike the strong hands of the woman who had comforted him as a child.

Or those of the young baker kneading another batch of dough beside him as he folded the last few pastries and transferred them to the baking sheet.

"Of course, Emma, you'll have to join us to keep the numbers even. And keep Papa distracted."

Why would a servant be invited to join a formal party? This was certainly an unusual household and his foray into the kitchens had become quite eye-opening. The longer he stayed quiet, the more he learned.

Beside him, Emma shook her head. "Nay. I cannot—"

"Yes. You can. You've done it before, so no arguments. And I'd like that bath delivered within a quarter hour."

As if hot water appeared by some magic fairy.

Emma patted the ball of dough now resting in the wooden bowl and turned her attention to the soaking apple slices. "I won't be doing any of your fetching this afternoon. There's a meal to prepare, and it's your own fault your ladies maid was let go this morn. You can ask one of the other maids or if you're in a hurry, you could take a pitcher of water and a simple tray with you now."

Miss Phoebe sputtered and shook her head. "I can't be seen carrying my own pitcher."

"You could always use the servant's stairs." Emma pointed toward a door he hadn't noticed before.

"Never." Miss Phoebe spun on her heel and left the way she came without either bath water or food.

Quiet descended in her wake. Grayson finished loading the tray with pastries while Emma sprinkled spices and sugar over the re-plumped apples.

But the other woman's intrusion had served to remind him of his mission. And his position, even as he longed to recapture the easy camaraderie of before if only for a few minutes.

He cleared his throat. "What's this about a stuffy old baron coming for dinner?"

Emma shrugged, but could not hide the uncomfortable emotion that flashed across her eyes. "I am not privy to the guest list, only the numbers. Which apparently now need to be adjusted once again."

Because if Miss Phoebe had her way, Emma would now be shedding her apron and dining with the others. Did she own a dinner gown?

"I'm curious. Most servants don't join the family and their guests for dinner."

She ducked her head and stirred the apples with a fierce pace. "Don't let appearances deceive you. I'm actually the poor orphaned cousin who was given a home out of charity."

Trying to find the resemblance, Grayson studied the rich tones of Emma's hair, her build, and even tried to recall the shape of her eyes. Aquamarine eyes that finally lifted to meet his.

"My father was the second son who died at sea, but my mother was also a relative of the late Lady Bainbridge."

"I'm sorry for your loss." He nodded, then swallowed his grief. Losing a father was a painful thing. And if she were truly orphaned, then they had both also lost their mothers.

Then again, from what he knew of Lord Bainbridge, the man's wife had died well over a year before, giving Grayson a touch of compassion for the spoiled Miss Phoebe trying to navigate courtship without her mother's advice.

But the fact Emma's mother had been in a position to marry a baron's younger son bespoke a genteel family of the sort who would happily betroth another of their daughters to a different baron. The sort of family he would have searched among for a bride of his own, if not for his satchel of papers sure to destroy his dreams.

The contemplative moment of shared grief was broken by the boisterous return of the cook leading a parade of assorted maids and footmen bearing picnic baskets and other burdens. The overlapping conversations quickly revealed the outcomes of multiple outings by the resident lord, his sister, and all three daughters.

Emma turned away and pulled the golden loaves of bread from the oven, then slid the tray of berry-filled pastries in their place. But before they could begin to assemble his special order, a large woman in a severe black dress entered down the servants' staircase.

With a brisk clapping of her hands, she captured everyone's attention and began barking orders to the collective mob of servants as only the head housekeeper could.

He glanced at Emma with a half-smile only to find her biting her lip and tilting her head back toward the main hallway. Giving him the obvious cue that it was time from him to leave the warmth of the kitchens behind and return to where he belonged before he got her into trouble.

Fighting disappointment, he strode to a basin to wash his hands before reclaiming his coat. And the satchel containing the physical reminder of his burdens.

At least he would get to see Emma again over a shared meal.

Chapter Four

A t the stroke of seven, Emma descended the grand staircase in one of Phoebe's cast-off gowns from the last season. After finishing the baking and repairing her cousin's damaged hem, other tasks had intruded leaving her precious little time to get herself ready in proper fashion.

Especially if she didn't wish to offend their hostess Lady Rowley, her widowed aunt on her father's side, with a display of poor manners from her household.

The bodice was a bit too tight for her tastes, however, the pale gold of the silk fabric managed to make her eyes appear more green than blue tonight. And although she hadn't the time or patience for an elaborate hairstyle, her unadorned hair showcased the warmer hues she'd inherited from her father.

Overall, she shouldn't *appear* too out of place at the dinner table.

If only she belonged alongside the other guests.

Her presence at the formal dinner would feel as uncomfortable as the itchy ruffles of lace at her elbows.

Emma paused at the foot of stairs to catch her breath, and after a quick prayer for courage, schooled her features into what she hoped was a serene expression. After a quick glance at the butler, who nodded his approval, she stepped into the drawing room.

Where her arrival went completely overlooked by her family and their guests.

Which shouldn't have been a surprise. After all, the only place she'd ever been noticed for making a fashionable entrance was in her dreams of King Arthur and his castle by the sea.

She glanced around the room at the elegantly garbed men and bejeweled women. Her uncle's wealth was on display around the necks of his three daughters and even his widowed sister had her own collection of glittering gems. And that was before the addition of two older couples and four single young men, most in clothing that easily cost more than a year's wages. Diamonds and rubies winked from the buttons and cuffs of the men while one of the other women even wore jeweled combs in her hair that matched her emerald choker.

Emma's hand darted to her bare neck, then fluttered back to her side. Of course, she'd left her mother's tin locket back in her room. And none had thought to loan her even a simple strand of pearls.

Feeling awkwardly out of place, Emma moved to a single chair along the wall where she could observe the interactions of the others and await the call to dinner. And having already been subjected to the giggles and speculation abovestairs about which eligible bachelor her cousins had their hopes set upon, it didn't take long to sort out the identities of the various guests.

While the three sisters were classically pretty in their own right, marriage contracts among the peers of the realm were usually based on business rather than love. And her uncle would make the most of any possible negotiations.

Cecilia, as the oldest and the most vivacious of the three, sat at the piano and seemed to have caught the attention of the Viscount Egerton, whose strawberry-loving mother watched from a nearby Chippendale armchair. While her uncle's title did not nearly compare to that of the talkative young man who would eventually inherit an earldom from his father, Lord Bainbridge's wealth and influence in the region promised both an ally and an ample dowry. Meanwhile, if the match were made, her cousin would get her wish to live closer to London.

On another chaise lounge, her poetry-loving cousin Julia visited quietly with the somber Mr. Newton, eldest son and heir to the Viscount Haddington with a seat near Exeter.

Even Phoebe's rapt conversation with the mere Mr. Smythe near the windows offered a potential advantage. Assuming the rumors of his family's alleged connections to the owners of the smuggling hotbed Jamaica Inn were true. Based upon the cut of his clothing and rich fabrics, her cousin would not lack any indulgence either should her wishes for the match prevail.

That left their mystery guest standing alone near the fireplace and shifting from one foot to the other. He'd exchanged his black jacket from earlier for one with ornate gold embroidery in keeping with a formal dinner party, but unlike the other men with their heavily powdered wigs, he had left his clean brown hair tied back with a simple black ribbon.

Just like her step-father used to do.

Her traitorous heart skipped a beat with longing. Yet, despite their time together in the kitchens, she could not approach their guest without benefit of a proper introduction. At least not without igniting a scandal that would reflect poorly on the rest of the Clarke family.

Although, if Phoebe had been able to sway her aunt regarding the seating arrangements, Emma might be paired with the gentlemen for the evening. Meaning the upcoming dinner might not be so uncomfortable after all.

A few minutes later, Lady Rowley broke away from her conversation with Lady Wexley and approached Emma with a frown. "I wish your cousin had thought to consult me before issuing her invitations."

Emma stood and smoothed the wrinkles from her gown. "Am I not needed then?" A strange stab of disappointment pierced her midsection.

The imperious woman shot a glare at Phoebe and Mr. Smythe. "Nay. I need the numbers. But you'll have to come along while I make the proper introductions."

Trailing in her wake, Emma relied on the rigid societal constructs and protocol to mask her nerves at being introduced to multiple peers of the realm at once. Powerful men who regularly debated the laws of the land and possibly even rubbed shoulders with the royal family.

As Lady Rowley paired the guests off for dinner, she finally motioned for the gentleman beside the fire to approach. "And Miss Phoebe, may I formally introduce Lord Danvers."

Emma sucked in a quick breath. No. It couldn't be.

"Sir Grayson Wentworth, at your service." He offered a slight bow.

Her young cousin dipped into a small curtsy, then raised an eyebrow and raked her gaze over their visitor as if assessing his worth as compared to her supposed beau. "Pleased to meet you, m'lord."

Others pushed forward to offer their expected condolences over the recent loss of his father and from the back of the cluster, Emma took a moment to study the handsome boy who had once played with her and the other village children before returning to his castle-like manor above the sea.

Above her village on the coast that she still longed for.

In the manor that until recently had been home to a stuffy old baron like the one Phoebe had scorned, especially after the death of his beloved wife in childbirth and then sending his lively son away to school.

Before further introductions could be made, the butler arrived to announce that dinner was served.

As the other guests began to proceed to the formal dining room, Lady Rowley quickly paired Emma with Mr. Smythe. Emma rested a hand on his bent elbow as they followed behind the others, eventually taking their assigned seats at the far end of the long table but across from Phoebe and Lord Danvers.

While the footmen served the first course, Emma peeked at the new baron. No wonder he had seemed familiar earlier.

Now that she wasn't ducking her head like a true servant should in the presence of her superiors or preoccupied with the baking, she easily recognized the distinctive color of his eyes.

Along with other clues like the slight scar on his cheek that brought back a wealth of memories from home when he'd been known locally only as the young Wentworth.

How could she have overlooked his mention of loving fruit-filled pastries as a boy? Emma had sometimes visited the kitchen where her mother worked after her step-father's accident and had been present at times when a much younger Wentworth had stopped by for an afternoon treat. Especially baked goods that had been made by her very own mother.

Once the soup had been served, the lavish room echoed with the clinks of silver spoons against fine porcelain. Eventually, a variety of conversations emerged again between the designated dining companions.

Except at her end of the table.

Increasingly uncomfortable at the silence, Emma turned to Mr. Smythe hoping to invite a conversation, but his attention was focused across the table. Where Phoebe kept sneaking glances back through her lowered lashes.

Emma gave a slight cough to remind her younger cousin of her etiquette lessons.

With a flushed face, Phoebe finally turned to her assigned companion and asked if he'd been to London since he'd assumed his father's title. As topics went, it was mildly inappropriate, but at least the new baron was able to pick up and shift the conversation elsewhere.

His off-hand comment about feeling the earthquake the last time he'd been near London, triggered additional conversations down the table about damaged buildings, howling dogs, and clanging church bells. It had been the second earthquake that year and there were those who preached God's judgment was at hand.

However the willingness to converse seemed to have skipped the wealthy but untitled man beside her who chose to eat in silence while staring at Phoebe.

Breaking all acceptable protocol, Emma finally asked if he had ever visited London.

Only to have him stare down his lifted nose as if she were something foul upon his shoe. "I've no interest in talking to charity cases."

Emma sucked in a quick breath, then despite the painful reminder of her position in the household, embraced a wave of relief as Phoebe's invited guest inserted himself into a conversation with the couple on his other side.

Leaving her to dine alone in peaceful obscurity as her soup bowl was removed and replaced with a clean plate for the next course. As platters of food were brought from the kitchen to be served, a somewhat heated debate erupted between two of the men further down the length of the banquet table.

It seemed that across the ocean France was expanding into areas controlled by the British colonies and some argued for a greater military presence there. If her father had still been alive, she wondered what his opinion would have been.

However, the topic of the colonies led a few women to exclaim their shock at the idea of unclothed savages while other men berated the backwoods colonials who complained about King George's policies with one breath but expected protection all the same.

Emma bit her lip. Her uncle was one who chastised the colonists for their complaints about foreign rule yet also turned a blind eye to the smugglers who circumvented other rules like the collection of taxes on his cellar full of contraband brandy.

She peeked at Lord Danvers and caught a glimpse of a vein ticking in his tensed jaw. Almost as if he was displeased with the discussion around them.

Had his years away at the university changed him? Although, based on his behavior earlier in the day, it didn't seem like he'd become as enamored with upholding the class structure as others in the room. Unlike her uncle whose grandfather had actually purchased their title but now expected everyone to treat him and his family as if he were on equal footing with others who inherited their status.

Like the Danvers title that had been initially granted to Richard Wentworth by King Henry VIII at the Battle of Spurs almost two hundred years before the Bainbridge title had come into existence. It was a tale everyone from Tintagel to Boscastle was familiar with.

Although after inheriting that legacy, the new Lord Danvers was as beyond her reach now as he had ever been in their childhood. Yet, despite their differences, God had seen fit to bring a little bit of home to Bainbridge Manor.

The man in question glanced up from his plate and caught her watching him. Heat rushed to her face and she quickly turned back to her meal to eat in silence.

At long last, their dishes were cleared and the dessert course was brought in. As she'd planned, each small plate held both a strawberry-filled and an apple-filled pastry along with a scoop of sweetened whipped cream.

Lady Rowley was the first to poke at the sugar-sprinkled desserts with a wrinkled nose. "What is this?"

The footman cleared his throat. "Summer pastries featuring either spiced apples or freshly picked strawberries."

"Strawberries? My favorite." The countess practically squealed her excitement as she picked up her fork. "You'll have to have your cook give mine the recipe."

Emma risked another glance at her pastry-making helper and found him savoring a bite of the apple version with a dreamy expression on his face.

Even before knowing his identity, she had gone out of her way to make his favorite. But now, the thought of doing something special for her childhood infatuation sent warmth flooding her chest and brought a smile to her face.

Her mother would have been thrilled to bake for young Wentworth again.

It was a taste of heaven...and the home he wished to recreate.

Grayson closed his eyes and let the flavors dance on his tongue. While he could tell from the consistency of the apples that they weren't fresh, the flaky pastry was exactly how he'd remembered from his youth.

Back when Mrs. Richards was alive and he used to sneak into the kitchen hoping for a treat...and later on, a glimpse at her pretty daughter. Such priceless memories wrapped up in a blanket of dough.

He opened his eyes and found his gaze captured by Emma's. Her eyes shone as if she knew exactly what he was thinking. As if she understood how a simple treat could mean so much.

He nodded to acknowledge their connection and a furious blush rose on her face before she looked down at her plate once again.

Beside him, Miss Phoebe snorted and poked her fork into the pastry. "These certainly are...rustic. I'm surprised the cook picked this for the menu."

Would she say the same if she knew he had helped? Probably not. And yet, it was likely a good thing she'd been so occupied with herself earlier in the kitchen that she didn't recognize him. And therefore couldn't make him look or feel any more foolish than he already did in this company.

He cast a quick glance from Emma's simple beauty across the table to the overly jeweled and curled presence of the woman beside him. And then further down the long table to her equally decorated sisters. All were lovely, yet the direct descendants of the resident baron appeared to enjoy flaunting their wealth.

Wealth he did not currently have since he'd spent almost everything fixing up the surrounding properties and abiding by the bequests in his father's will. He'd even sold many of his mother's jewels, saving only a strand of her pearls to give to his betrothed in good faith.

Yet, even if he had the coin, he could not compete with at least two of the other young men in the room. He actually knew both Egerton and Newton from Cambridge, although they had been a few years ahead of him and easily overlooked the Wentworth boy from the pirate shores. Even the legendary exploits of Sir Francis Drake and Sir Richard Grenville from the Cornwall coast had not made up for his comparative lack of title.

Not even the occasional box of somewhat stale pastries from home had been able to erase that lingering sense of isolation.

With a sigh, Grayson turned his attention back to the deliciously fresh pastries on his plate. No sense wallowing in regret.

At the other end of the table, the countess continued to rave about the berry pastries. "Wexley, darling, these would be ideal to serve during our Midsummer's Eve celebration."

Beside him, Miss Phoebe lowered her voice. "That is where this supposed dessert belongs." She cast a pointed glare at her cousin. "Not in the present company."

Emma merely bit her lip and endured the criticism.

Thankfully, the mention of the upcoming festival managed to shift the topic of conversation from politics, wars, taxes, and smugglers...to their expected obligations toward the people under their responsibility.

Hopefully his own people would not be disappointed by a reduced menu and festivities. Then again, over the past month, they all know how much he had invested into the general upkeep of the area. Perhaps they would be content with a simpler celebration this summer and a larger one come Christmas. After the harvest had refilled his coffers.

Out of the corner of his eye, he caught Emma motioning a footman closer, then whispering something into his ear with a covert glance toward him and then down the table to the strawberry-loving countess.

Before he could discern Emma's purpose, the baron's sister rose and led the feminine retreat toward the drawing room while the men lingered behind. A footman poured glasses of port or brandy, but Grayson chose another cup of tea instead.

And endured a round of teasing as a result before he became the focus of the sort of placating and pandering attention he could see a mile away. Especially with a clear head.

Since inheriting the title after his father's passing, Grayson was officially an equal in the House of Lords. But that didn't keep him from feeling out of his element or prevent the older generation at the table from pointing out that he still had a lot to learn and would be wise to follow their lead.

Then again, their generation was already experienced with the upkeep of their estates and the execution of various contracts such as those he had learned about at Cambridge.

And those he'd uncovered in his father's desk.

He squirmed at the uncomfortable reminder of the papers he had brought with him. It was almost time to get down to business with the baron.

After waiting for Lord Bainbridge to finish his second glass of brandy, Grayson waved a hand to get the man's attention. "My lord, may I have a few minutes in private?"

The Earl of Wexley chuckled and nudged his son in the side. "You need a turn later, too?"

Grayson's face heated as he squirmed under the additional scrutiny. "I came across some unfinished business among my father's papers and need to—"

"If it's your father's business, we cannot begrudge you the time." The Viscount Haddington nodded his approval.

As if anything Grayson needed personally was not worthy of the baron's valuable time at the expense of his guests. As if Grayson himself was not worthy to be numbered among those guests.

Lord Bainbridge grunted, then stood. "Gentlemen, finish your brandy and rejoin the ladies when you're ready. We'll only be a few minutes." With a nod at Grayson, he turned and led the way across the entry hall and down a short corridor.

Once inside his dark-paneled private study, the baron lit several candles, then strode around his desk and took a seat on a large leather chair. Grayson paused only to close the door before pulling up a chair opposite the desk.

"I was surprised to get your note because I hadn't spoken to your father in years. Whatever could we have to talk about now?"

"Actually, I have two items to discuss." Grayson took a deep breath as he pulled the leather pouch of papers from his inner jacket pocket and removed two pieces of parchment. "First, when going through my father's papers to settle the estate, I came upon this letter and a blank betrothal contract."

Grayson reluctantly handed the sheets across the desktop. "Apparently, the two of you had agreed that I was to marry one of your daughters once we were of age."

Lord Bainbridge frowned as he studied the papers.

"While he never said anything to me about this while he was alive, a Wentworth always keeps his word." Grayson shifted on his chair. "Apparently my father had already drawn up a contract. All that remains is the inclusion of a name for the bride, a dowry amount, and our signatures."

"I'd forgotten all about this." A variety of emotions flitted across the other man's face. "Presently, I have other offers to consider for my daughters." He waved a beefy hand back in the direction of the dining room, making his point abundantly clear.

Grayson shifted on his chair. "I understand. But I had to—"

"That said, I am willing to consider your suit if the terms are right." Lord Bainbridge raised an assessing gaze to Grayson as if finally taking his measure as a man.

If the terms were right? "Sir, whatever happened to honoring your word?"

"This has your father's signature on it, not mine. How serious are *you* about uniting our households?" The older baron smirked.

Grayson's stomach churned to have his loyalty to his father's wishes questioned. On the one hand, it would be easy enough to let the issue slide and the presumed betrothal fall by the wayside, allowing him to find his own bride on his own terms.

But that was his father's signature and the scrawled letters spelled out Lord Danvers. His name now, placing his personal integrity at stake. And despite the way he'd been treated earlier in the dining room, he was not a whelp of a boy incapable of making a life-changing decision for himself.

Lord Bainbridge chuckled and pushed the parchment aside. "I thought so. You're too—"

"How serious am I about honoring my father's word? This serious." Grayson reached for inkstand near the center of the baron's desk. After dipping the quill into the ink, he snatched the contract and signed his name on the line before sliding the contract back across the smooth surface. "Now, what are *you* going to do about it?"

Lord Bainbridge simply raised one eyebrow as he took the pen and dipped it in the ink. The tip hovered over the line naming the bride for a moment, then retreated. "Let us wait a bit to be sure."

"Wait?" Grayson's breath caught in his throat.

"Yes. I need time to think what will be best." The man raised an eyebrow. "A merger with an estate on the coast could lead to a favorable trade agreement that would benefit us both."

Grayson suppressed his internal cringe. The only trade he'd heard of lately involved smugglers and the newly built Jamaica Inn. He'd rather not have the Danvers name anywhere near that line of business on the wrong side of the law even if others along the rugged coast lured unsuspecting ships onto the rocks and looted their holds.

"But my daughters' happiness is also at stake. So, yes, we wait." He replaced the quill into the inkstand. "I think you might have a chance with my youngest daughter. I'll arrange an outing on the morrow to see if you suit."

The youngest? Miss Phoebe was the last woman he wanted to be shackled to for the rest of his life. He struggled to hide his churning emotions while his fingers itched to grab the quill and scratch through his signature thereby voiding the contract.

Like an impulsive fool trying to prove his worth after an evening of being overlooked or pandered to, he'd jumped ahead.

Before he could ask for the contract back, there was a shuffling noise outside the door followed by a knock.

"Come in." Lord Bainbridge called out the welcome and Newton and his father Lord Haddington immediately entered. "Stop by tomorrow afternoon after your outing, and we'll talk more about this matter." The baron waved Grayson out of his chair, then locked the signed contract in his desk before standing to greet the newcomers.

Grayson gritted his teeth at being so quickly dismissed. Especially before being able to discuss the second matter that had brought him to Whitstone. But for the moment, his bruised ego could only take so much abuse.

While he slipped out the door of the library, he spotted Lord Wexley and Egerton also lingering nearby. Was it wrong to hope the other men's suits won out so he could escape Whitstone with his integrity intact?

If only he didn't need a wife's dowry to cover the manor's expenses until harvest. Especially after he handled the rest of his father's business.

A constricting band tightened around his chest. He was surely trapped by both his father's will and his obligation to the throne to oversee the region of Danvers. And now he was equally bound by his personal signature on the folded contract in the other man's desk.

How had things gone from bad to worse so quickly? And why hadn't he thought to pray before signing?

Chapter Five

Chapter 5

Emma spread orange marmalade across a slice of spiced bread and stifled a yawn. Admittedly, her sleep had been disrupted with romantic dreams of a handsome new baron and King Arthur's Tintagel, but with the morning light, the reality of her position had once again intruded.

She took a sip of tea and vowed to stop wasting time dwelling on the impossible.

At the other end of the breakfast table under the watchful eye of their aunt, Cecilia and Julia continued to discuss the dinner party and replay the same conversations Emma had endured from the isolated perimeter of the drawing room.

To be so close to family and still excluded from their experiences was often the worst sort of torture. It might have been better to stay in Danvers and marry a fisherman than have been uprooted and brought to Whitstone only to linger on the fringes.

Except it hadn't always been that way. At least at the beginning, Lady Bainbridge had tried to comfort her in her grief and promised a debut experience like those of her two oldest daughters. However, it was on a shopping excursion to secure fabrics for Emma's new wardrobe that her carriage overturned and the lady lost her life.

And Emma had lost her advocate as her motherless cousins clung to each other and her uncle blamed her for putting his wife in harm's way. Once their year of mourning was past, the baron's—and her father's—widowed sister had moved back home and the only debut ever discussed was Phoebe's.

"Good news, girls." Her uncle's booming voice intruded as he burst into the room with an uncharacteristically wide smile.

"What?"

"Tell us."

"Don't keep them in suspense." Lady Rowley merely raised an eyebrow but something in her tone reminded Emma of a cat lapping up a bowl of cream.

The baron instructed a footman to prepare his plate, then strode to his usual place at the head of the table. "Julia? Haddington and I have reached an agreement."

A dreamy smile spread across her middle cousin's face while Cecilia squealed loudly.

Lord Bainbridge pointed a finger at his middle daughter. "I've instructed your ladies maid to begin packing. You and your aunt will be leaving within the hour to visit their estate and begin arrangements for a wedding to start the season."

"So soon?" Her dreamy tone faded as Julia sat up tall.

Lady Rowley patted her hand. "His grandfather, the Earl of Gladstone, is fading and it won't be long until your Mr. Newton advances in rank. It's wise to solidify the bond before he decides to set his sights higher."

Julia flinched at the reminder that despite the family's wealth, she was the middle daughter of a rural baron.

Which was still a far cry higher in prospects than being the orphaned daughter of the second son.

"Just so." The baron grunted, then turned to his eldest daughter. "You and I are also leaving shortly for a similar visit."

"To Wexley?" A hopeful smile spread across Cecilia's face.

"Precisely. The earl and I must finalize the negotiations, but Egerton wished to introduce you to the rest of his family." Another squeal erupted and her uncle clapped his hands over his ears. "Have mercy."

"I apologize for my unladylike response." Cecilia uttered the proper words, but her gleeful expression never faded.

"He sent over a note this morning that it's as good as done. Seems his mother's opinion was the deciding vote, but the strawberry pastries at dinner and a box of leftovers was enough to tip the scale in our favor."

Lady Rowley wrinkled her nose. "Who would have thought it?"

Emma grinned at her cousins' joy. All because she had paid attention at the village warehouse, then had the opportunity to help in the kitchen, decide on the dessert, and then share the extra pastries.

And for her contribution, she'd had to endure barbs of criticism from one cousin while securing the future of another.

God, You see me, right?

Her uncle turned his attention to his own breakfast as excited chatter erupted between her cousins and their aunt. The room was filled with high-pitched mentions of wedding dates, trousseau shopping, and dressmaker appointments.

There would be an exhausting flurry of wedding activity and arrangements ahead. Then, before she knew it, Phoebe would be the only one left to secure a match. And if her Mr. Smythe declared his intentions, within the year her cousins could all have households elsewhere and Emma would no longer be needed to aid in their matches or care.

Then what would she do? And where would she go?

In the middle of the happy chaos, Phoebe stumbled into the room with a yawn. "What's all the fuss?"

"I'm engaged—"

"And I'm practically there too."

"What about me?" Phoebe's bottom lip jutted out as she took a seat at the table.

Cecilia smirked. "Stop being the baby trying to tag along. You'll get your turn eventually."

Julia nodded. "For now, simply enjoy the attention as the only unattached Clarke daughter."

Her uncle chuckled. "Actually, I'm considering an offer for Phoebe's hand as well."

The other three women burst into speculation, pleading with the baron for details. It seemed that only Emma caught the flash of confusion and then panic on Phoebe's face.

Of course, hearing you were to be married had to be both thrilling and petrifying at the same time. Something that—without a dowry—Emma would never get to experience at the same level.

Her uncle held up his hands. "I sent a note for Lord Danvers to come mid-morning for an outing with Phoebe to get better acquainted."

"Can't you entertain him?" Phoebe's voice held more than a hint of a whining tone as a footman set a small plate before her. "I've already accepted an invitation from Mr. Smythe."

"No. I'm not available. The rest of us are leaving this morn and won't return until Saturday afternoon."

Leaving Emma almost three full days with only one cousin to assist. It would be a welcome calm before the storm of wedding preparations.

Although based on the noise in the hall outside the breakfast room, other staff members were already in a scurry to carry out the baron's instructions on time.

"You'll have to entertain your guest yourself." The baron pushed aside his plate and reached for his cup of tea.

"Do I have to?" Well-practiced tears welled and then spilled over onto Phoebe's pink cheeks.

Her uncle shifted in his chair and a long-suffering sigh emerged. The man always grew uncomfortable around tears. A fact his daughters—especially Phoebe—exploited on occasion. "Yes. His father and I had discussed an alliance long ago and I can't afford to make an enemy."

Phoebe glanced down the table toward Emma's chair. "If I have to entertain him, can I at least bring Emma along to help?"

Her stomach churned over the drama Phoebe was known for...and the uncomfortably pleasant surge of hope that she might get to spend additional time with the man who had recaptured her attention.

However, should it be arranged, her purpose in that encounter would be clear. To protect Phoebe's reputation while helping secure the best match possible for the young woman's future.

Part of her hoped the young man didn't get saddled with her emotional cousin for life...while another voice scolded her disloyalty to her family.

Had Lord Danvers truly offered for her younger cousin or was her uncle hoping to wring an offer from him? Was he still unattached and if so, would Emma herself have a chance?

No. The foolish dreams of Tintagel had clouded her judgment and robbed her of both sleep and proper perspective. She'd been tempted to imagine things were different. As if she'd traveled the countryside. Been to London. Had a debut.

But with no realistic chance at a romance, she'd be better off contemplating how to tell Lord Danvers that she was originally from the village by the sea.

Because once her cousins were all married, maybe he would give her a job at his castle where at least she could see and smell the sea again. Even if she needed to spend her days knowing he was married to another woman.

Emma took another sip of her cooling tea and prayed for wisdom.

Of course, approaching the young baron for a private conversation could be misunderstood as an inappropriate flirtation and destroy her reputation. Perhaps she should bring up the topic in front of Phoebe? No. The brash girl was likely to share Emma's plans with her father and cause unnecessary trouble.

Emma would need to tread carefully. But at least their aunt would be gone instead of watching over all of the interactions like a hawk.

"Let's go."

Emma jolted from her thoughts as Phoebe pulled her to her feet. The others were already leaving the breakfast room and the footmen had begun clearing the dishes.

Had she truly been so lost in thought that she'd missed the fact her day's activities had been decided? Or would Phoebe take advantage of her distraction?

With another prayer for patience, Emma followed Phoebe up the stairs toward the family's wing of bedrooms.

"Without Molly to help, I had to wait for Julia's maid to assist me into my gown and that's why I was late to breakfast."

An unfortunate consequence of Phoebe's actions firing her maid over an imperfect job with the irons. Would her cousin learn from her mistake and hold her tongue in the future? Not likely.

"But now that they're all traveling, we're short on maids and you'll have to help me change before this morning's outing."

So much for a few days to relax.

Emma sighed when they reached Phoebe's room and she spied the emptied wardrobe and pile of discarded dresses strewn across her unmade bed.

Thanks to Phoebe's ever-shifting moods, Emma would be spending the next hours tidying the room, doing up buttons, and styling hair. She shot a glance at herself in the mirror above the vanity table. Emma's own simple gown and loosely pulled-back hair would have to suffice for her morning's role as a companion.

With quick hands, Emma busied herself with the necessary tasks. All the while listening to her cousin alternately pout and rant.

The girl had wanted a prestigious offer like her sisters had received. And yet in the same breath wished that her precious Francis would have declared himself last night. Except that her father had been in his study with the other men for so long that the man she loved had called for his horse and gone home instead.

But the worst of her opinions were reserved for the not-so-old but oh-so-unwelcome Lord Danvers.

Emma flinched as one of Phoebe's shoes hit the opposite wall.

"Did you see how he was dressed? His clothes were mostly unadorned and he didn't even bother with a powdered wig. It was a formal dinner party, but if he couldn't make the effort either he's uncouth or he doesn't have the money. Especially compared to my Francis." A pillow joined her shoe beside the wall. "I only hope I don't get stuck with Lord Danvers and have to move to some ugly house."

"Actually, Wentworth Manor is quite lovely." Emma had been privileged to step inside during former Midsummer's Eve and Twelfth Night celebrations in addition to trailing along with her mother to work on occasion.

Phoebe scowled. "Then you marry the stiff."

Emma's heart skipped a beat under the weight of her longing for home and the memory of those amazing eyes filled with mischief.

Lord, forgive me for my jealousy.

For the second day in a row, Grayson trotted his horse through the iron gates leading to Bainbridge Manor.

The baron had sent a note that morning instructing him when to arrive in order to entertain Miss Phoebe. The note lay in the pocket of his coat alongside his packet of other papers, not for sentimental reasons but simply for safekeeping out of the prying eyes of the vicar's wife.

Eating his breakfast at their small table had been enough of an exercise in patience. Thankfully the vicar had joined him and the conversation had been split between Grayson's questions seeking insight into the region's political issues and Mrs. Pembroke's ceaseless chatter relaying the village gossip about an earl, a viscount, and a baron all staying within their borders.

She had cast a glance at her husband and tried to frown over the fact that some were laying wagers as to which daughter would be married first and to whom. Grayson's struggle to keep a straight face and not inquire about her opinion had quickly disappeared when her gaze turned sympathetic. As if he didn't stand a chance against the competition.

Which could yet be a blessing in disguise if he was freed to pursue his own heart. That option had gained more traction last night when the stable boy had handed him the reins for his horse...and a box of extra apple pastries.

Obviously something the lovely Emma had arranged for his benefit.

He nudged his horse forward in anticipation, then recalled who he was officially there to see and suppressed a shudder. Hopefully he'd caught Miss Phoebe on a bad day yesterday, but feared he was only lying to himself.

The memory of Mrs. Pembroke's wrinkled nose and mutter of "that Miss Phoebe" rattled his nerves along with the clatter of hooves on cobblestones. It seemed the vicar's wife was of the opinion the girl had been overly pampered and sheltered and had some growing up yet to do.

Would such a woman ever be capable of running an entire household with the decorum and frugality that Danvers needed?

There was only one way to find out.

Grayson dismounted and handed the care of his horse off to a stable boy before climbing the stairs. Today, a footman swung the door open before he had even arrived at the top.

Once inside, he removed his cocked hat. "I have an appointment to speak with Miss Phoebe, but I would also like to make arrangements to speak with the baron—"

"You've just missed him, m'lord."

Grayson blinked. He didn't think he had passed anyone on the road from Whitstone.

The footman grinned like he was relaying the juiciest of gossip. "Lord Bainbridge is off to finalize an engagement."

"For whom?" His stomach clenched. Of course both Lord Egerton and Mr. Newton had been present last evening along with their parents. Not to mention that local merchant's son Mr. Smythe.

The footman leaned forward and lowered his voice. "You didn't hear it from me, but both Miss Clarke and Miss Julia are spoken for."

Already? Apparently the baron had moved fast on some offers while dragging his feet where the Danvers estate was concerned.

Grayson's stomach twisted into a knot. "When will his lordship return?"

"He is expected back Saturday afternoon." The man held out a hand to take Grayson's hat.

And today was Thursday with chances of conducting any business on Saturday evening unlikely and Sunday frowned upon. Leaving him with long days spent waiting for the man to return so he could finish his business in the area. It didn't seem prudent to return home only to venture back a few days later.

No. He would have to exercise patience and spend another few nights at the Whitstone vicar's house since he hadn't been invited to stay at the manor and could not presume upon their hospitality.

Of course, he could make arrangements to stay at the inn, but it was likely simpler to face the scrutiny he knew than go another round with the sharp-tongued innkeeper's wife. Not to mention the additional expense.

"Miss Clarke is awaiting your arrival in the drawing room."

Grayson pushed aside all concerns over lodging and followed the footman toward the inevitable meeting with his potential bride. The sole remaining option.

A high-pitched giggle echoed out into the hall and once again he regretted his hasty actions with a pen. Although his father's signature was sufficiently binding even before Lord Bainbridge's taunting.

Grayson swallowed hard against the tightening bonds of his future, and with a deep breath for courage, he stepped into the room and scanned the occupants.

Miss Phoebe in a lavish day gown posed prettily on a chaise lounge while the same Mr. Smythe from last evening's dinner hovered nearby. What was he doing there? Yet in the kitchen, hadn't Grayson heard from her own lips about their secret engagement? Could it be true?

"Oh, Lord Danvers. You've arrived." Miss Phoebe fluttered her eyelashes in presumed innocence, then glanced between him and her other suitor with a half smile. "I'm sorry to convey that I had already made plans before my father announced your intentions to visit today. I'm sure you won't mind being an additional member in our party."

He blinked. What was a man supposed to say to that?

The young woman giggled again. "Don't worry. You won't be alone. I've invited Emma to join us for a stroll through the gardens."

He followed her gaze to find Emma near the windows looking awkwardly out of place in another simple gown. He nodded a greeting, then stepped closer as if drawn beyond his will. "Good day, Miss..." Miss what? Had he ever been officially introduced to her?

Another annoying laugh interrupted his thoughts. "There are too many Miss Clarkes in this house already. You can just call her Emma."

The woman in question closed her eyes for a moment as bracing up her courage. Or biting her tongue.

He waited until she opened her eyes, then raised an eyebrow in question.

She nodded with a soft smile. "Just Emma is fine."

After yesterday's interlude in the kitchen, he felt a similar need to be informal. Even though he could hear Miss Phoebe flirting with Mr. Smythe as if trying to soothe his ruffled feelings, Grayson lowered his voice. "I'm still not sure when I'll answer to Danvers without looking around for my father, so if you like, you can call me Wentworth."

Her smile grew. "I understand your confusion over a name."

What? Now he was additionally confused, but before he could question her further, she rested a hand on his sleeve.

"I'm sorry for your loss, m'lord. Your father was a—"

"Emma? Are you ready to go?" Miss Phoebe's sharp tone broke them apart.

What had Emma been about to say? Did she know his father or only know of him? And yet her sympathy had triggered his own emotions to the point he welcomed the distraction as her cousin led them all out the double doors to the gardens.

However, once they were outside, Miss Phoebe pulled Mr. Smythe close enough to whisper something in his ear. Grayson gritted his teeth as the man responded to her actions with an arm around her waist and a roving hand that seemed to be welcomed since his actions were received with another giggle as the baron's daughter guided their foursome deeper into the hedged walkways.

Leaving him paired with Emma and trailing behind.

Beside him, she cleared her throat. "Can you tell me, how is Wentworth Manor these days?"

It was the type of polite conversation that should matter or be of interest to the woman who might become his wife. If Miss Phoebe was listening.

But since home was his favorite place of all, he began to talk of his homecoming after years away. Which inevitably brought up the number of changes that had occurred including the necessary reduction in the household staff and the absence of his favorites from his childhood.

A sniffle from Emma drew his attention and he caught the pain in her eyes before she glanced away toward her cousin. As if she wasn't allowed to feel grief when the current household had suffered their own losses.

With a slight shake of her head, Emma pasted a smile on her face and shifted the conversation. "And Danvers? Are they still a friendly village of fisherman or has mining taken over?"

Something about her questions felt personal, almost as though she'd once visited the area or was interested in someone who lived there. Did she have her own suitor to consider?

He gazed down into Emma's lovely eyes that were reminiscent of a tide pool today, then was distracted by a strand of dark hair blowing across her smooth cheek. With this much poise in a simple dress, how would she conduct herself if attired in a lavish gown and bedecked with jewels?

No. He really must stop thinking of such things. He'd made a promise to his dying father and would honor the letter to the resident baron.

He shifted his gaze away from Emma's serene beauty and pretended to focus on the lavish gardens instead. After all, he was practically engaged to her cousin and needed the dowry money to support the needs of his estate, especially after funding the much needed repairs to the harbor's sea wall.

Could he really marry for money like so many of his class? He'd never thought to find himself in such a predicament and squirmed under the implications of letting his financial situation determine his course of action.

"My lord? Wentworth?" Emma's soft voice called him back to the present.

He scrambled to recall her question, then cleared his throat. "The villagers are a hard-working sort and very loyal. I wish I could give them the type of Midsummer's Eve celebration I remember from my childhood, but this transition has not been without it's trouble."

"I'm sorry to hear that, but I'm sure they are understanding."

"They have been." Despite his resolve, he found his heart touched by her compassionate insight.

Too tempted to continue a private conversation with Emma when he was there for her cousin, he deliberately raised his voice. "Miss Clarke, what can you tell me about your family's gardens?"

The woman he was supposed to be spending time with paused with a slight turn that invited him closer. Soon, he was strolling beside her down the next path and trying to ignore Mr. Smythe's angry glare on her other side.

The minutes ticked by in agonizing slowness as Miss Phoebe flirted with them both as if enjoying the attention and potential conflict. Behind them, Emma shrunk further into the background.

Despite his resolve to focus his attention on the baron's daughter, he counted down the minutes until their excursion was over and he could politely take his leave. Sparring with Mrs. Pembroke was a much better use of his time.

But a Wentworth always kept his word.

So he would have to be firm about a private outing tomorrow in order to give Miss Phoebe a fair chance.

After all, if they must marry, he should find something to admire about her.

And forget about the lovely Emma. Otherwise, he might be tempted to sacrifice his honor in the name of love.

Chapter Six

F riday morning, Emma was occupied ironing the floral-patterned skirt of one of Phoebe's muslin gowns when the head housekeeper tracked her down.

"Emma, this isn't your place." A frown creased Mrs. Carey's stern face.

"With Molly fired and the others away assisting my other cousins, Phoebe insisted I fill in to help her with her clothing."

The woman released a heavy sigh. "I'll find a replacement, but in the meantime, Mr. Stafford is asking for you."

Emma set aside the hot iron, then tightened the bow on her borrowed apron. "Of course. Where can I find him?"

"Leave the apron here." Her narrowed eyes drifted across Emma's hair and threadbare dress. "Pity you have no time to change, but he's already awaiting you near the drawing room."

Ah, yes. Lord Danvers was expected to call on Phoebe and someone had to stand watch over the couple.

A few minutes later, Emma exited the servants' passage into the main hall and shut the hidden door behind her. A moment later, the butler was by her side.

"Miss Emma, what should I do? Lord Danvers has arrived to take Miss Phoebe out for a ride, but she ordered the curricle brought around early." He lowered his voice but that didn't disguise his concern. "She drove off not a half hour ago with Mr. Smythe. I overheard him say that he'd packed a picnic, so I know she'll be gone most of the day."

Emma drew a quick breath. This time her cousin had gone too far. In addition to brazenly sneaking off unchaperoned with a suitor while her father and aunt were both away for a few days, her evasive actions were deliberately rude to the young baron.

After all, Emma had been standing not ten feet away yesterday when her cousin had batted her eyelashes and accepted his invitation to call.

Now Emma's stomach churned at the inevitable arguments once her uncle returned and his daughter's actions were reported. But in the meantime, what was to be done?

She could regretfully inform Lord Danvers of the change in plans and send him away, but she'd heard from her uncle's lips the desire not to make an enemy of him. Besides, Wentworth did not deserve such disregard.

The butler cleared his throat. "Miss?"

She sighed. "For the sake of my uncle's reputation, I'll need to entertain him myself and pray Lord Danvers does not take offense at the replacement." And pray she did not get any more romantic notions in her head.

A small smile flitted across Mr. Stafford's face. "You're just like your father, doing what's right no matter the challenge."

"My father?" Emma's gaze darted to the older servant. "You knew him?"

"Of course, miss. My family has served the Clarkes for generations and I always admired young Master Hugh when we were boys."

Longing stirred in her belly. "I'd love to hear more about him sometime if—"

"Ahem." Near the foot of the stairs, the housekeeper stood frowning.

Right. Emma was never to interact with the staff, especially when there were other tasks to be seen to.

Mr. Stafford cleared his throat. "As to entertaining the baron, will you be going out? I can have another carriage brought round."

Emma sighed at the lost opportunity to learn more about her father and turned her attention to the task ahead. "No. I think it would be simpler to stay in." Emma smoothed her hair back from her face while her foolish heart regretted not taking more care with her appearance that morn.

"Shall I have tea delivered?" Mr. Stafford's eyes swept over her face with another hint of approval.

Tea at this hour? It was far too early, but the serving would give her something to do during the coming encounter.

Emma nodded her acceptance of the butler's practical suggestion. "Yes, please."

As the butler left to issue the order, Emma moved toward the drawing room.

God, grant me the courage to do this by myself. Let him not be angry. And, oh, keep my heart secure in You.

She paused in the doorway to observe the man pacing beside the windows overlooking the gardens. While made of quality fabric, the simple lines of his jacket emphasized his height and the width of his shoulders, while his breeches hugged the muscles in his legs.

Heat rushed to her face as she raised her gaze and stepped into the room. "Good day, m'lord."

He pivoted and his eyes brightened at the sight of her, before looking beyond her to the empty doorway.

Emma willed her knees to support her as she moved further into the lavishly appointed room.

"She's running late?" The confusion on Wentworth's face gave her pause.

"She's not coming." Emma bit her lip as a flash of anger sparked in his eyes.

"Why not?"

"She did not say." Her shaking legs held her upright long enough to reach the nearest cluster of chairs.

A moment later, he joined her. "Is she here?"

A quick shake of her head was all she could manage. *God, help me make this right.* She cleared her throat. "I only just learned that she left a half hour ago and is expected to be gone most of the day."

His shoulders slumped. "What did I do? I'm trying to do the right thing to honor the agreement between our fathers."

"It's not you." Emma pressed her lips together to keep from speaking badly about her cousin.

Why couldn't Phoebe see the treasure before her?

Handsomeness aside, intelligence shone from his eyes and she'd already found Wentworth to be an attentive listener during their walk yesterday. He might not be as flamboyant as Mr. Smythe, but he was steady and reliable. And while he wasn't above spending time with the servants in the kitchen, he was born to be a leader and carried himself with integrity.

Oh, you foolish girl. Stop thinking of him thus.

Near at hand, Wentworth studied Emma's face. "You must know her well. What can I do to get her attention?"

"I've only lived here a little over two years, but I know that she enjoys receiving gifts."

He frowned. "I can't afford many gifts right now. I'm still putting the estate back in order after my father's prolonged illness."

"I'd heard of his passing, but not of his illness." It was her turn to frown. Hopefully the baron had not suffered overmuch.

"He spent a lot of coin on doctors, but in the end nothing would help. I'm doing my best with what resources remain, but until the harvest, caring for Danvers is my priority and main responsibility."

Her heart softened further. "As it should be. The villagers will depend on your leadership and knowing that you've invested in them before yourself will earn their loyalty. Or at the least the loyalty of the ones that matter."

A flash of admiration flickered in his eyes as if she had soothed a raw spot. Her pulse fluttered. Her beloved community was in capable hands.

"I pray my future wife will be so understanding because I've had to make sacrifices at the manor itself in order—"

A discrete cough announced the arrival of their tea. Emma glanced up to find the butler waiting nearby with raised eyebrows as he glanced between her and their guest who flushed as if embarrassed at his admission.

Welcoming the distraction, Emma stood. "Thank you, Mr. Stafford." She directed him to place the tray on a nearby table and then busied herself pouring out.

"How do you take your tea?"

An odd look crossed Wentworth's face again before he answered.

Tea wasn't normally served at this time of day, but he accepted the offered cup with a nod. As if also accepting her attempt to show the family's hospitality and not faulting her for her cousin's behavior.

Settling back onto her chair with a cup, Emma steered the conversation toward safer topics like the weather and assorted happenings in the village of Whitstone.

But halfway through her cup, Wentworth brought the conversation back to his question about how to capture Phoebe's attention. "If I can't afford expensive gifts, what else can I do to advance our necessary courtship?"

Emma grimaced. "I would say to spend time with her…"

"Which only works if she's here and I don't honestly have a lot of time to spend either."

"It's the quality not the quantity." Her voice cracked as the memories of her parents intruded.

He raised an eyebrow, obviously picking up on her tender emotions. "Come now, Emma. What do you mean?" He scooted his chair closer until she felt the depth of his concern and true interest.

If only he could fill the empty hole in her chest. "I already told you my father was the baron's younger brother."

"The second son who went to sea."

"Who sent back expensive gifts from various ports but was never home. Granted, I was quite young when he died, but I had no memories of him to hold onto. Just the color of my hair, my build, and a pile of dusty trinkets that my mother had to eventually sell in order to put food on our table."

"I'm sorry to pry."

She waved a hand to dismiss his apology. "Actually, I say that only to set up this. She eventually remarried but this time to a tin miner." She smiled at the precious memories. "We still didn't have much in the way of money but we were very happy as a family." She fingered the locket at her throat. "He gave her this and she wore it every day. Even though he was weary from his labor at the mine, he always came home with a smile on his face and asked me about my day. He took an interest in me and not just because the law said he was my guardian, but because he truly cared."

She paused as the memories intruded.

"And then?" Wentworth leaned forward as if sensing her story was about to change.

She sighed and set aside her empty cup before clasping her hands on her lap. "And then there was a horrible accident at the mine."

"An accident?" Grayson shook his head. Of course accidents happened at the mines. He still recalled the aftermath of one near Danvers that took the lives of several men and permanently maimed others. "Did he die too?"

"Not then." Tears welled in her eyes. "But he was unable to continue working. I was of an age to help fetch and care for him at home while my mother hired out for work. His body was broken, but he didn't get bitter. Without being able to offer any physical gifts whatsoever, he continually showed us his love for another six years before he too died when I was fourteen."

He winced at the way her voice wavered over her loss and sought to change the subject. "What about your mother? What was she like?"

The pain in her eyes disappeared beneath a warmth that stirred something in his heart. "I have her eyes, but I'd like to believe I have her personality as well. She taught me how to bake. But mostly she wasn't afraid of hard work, seeing it as a way to serve others and demonstrate God's love in action. Even after a long day up the hill, she always returned home with a smile."

Emma reached up to finger her mother's locket, an action he'd seen her do several times already. He had seen similar trinkets growing up near the mines and knew their true value lay in the sentiment, not the metal itself.

He took another sip of his rapidly-cooling tea. "And then?"

"When her second husband died, she vowed to never remarry. She died during an outbreak of small pox over two years ago." She offered a small smile. "While I know that she was exposed to the illness by nursing others in our village, I can't help but believe she'd lived too long with the loneliness of a broken heart and had already lost her will to live."

Her face twisted with raw emotion and he quickly glanced away, giving her the privacy to gather herself. But that didn't erase the glimpse of stark longing he'd observed when she talked of her mother's happy marriage.

It mirrored his own memories of his mother.

He coughed slightly, then shifted the conversation again. "And that's when you came here to live with family and receive their comfort."

"Perhaps at first, but too quickly thereafter, my cousins also lost their mother."

Compassion swelled in his chest. "As have I. Grief has touched us all, but your feelings are just as important as theirs."

She sat taller in her chair as she regained the rest of her composure. "I had forgotten about your mother. What do you remember of her?"

"I was ten when she died." Now it was his turn to stare into his half-empty cup as the memories flooded back. "She was the heart and soul of our home. And the inspiration behind the festivities whenever we invited the villagers to the manor for a Midsummer's Eve or Twelfth Night celebration."

"What was so special about her in your eyes?"

Grayson turned to look at Emma and found genuine care in her expression. "I'd forgotten some of the good things, but she always took time to listen to my stories about my adventures with the local boys. While I had a nanny, my mother always took time to read to me from the Bible and listened to my bedtime prayers. And she loved to play the piano and sing. At least until those last months."

He paused to collect his thoughts, but Emma let the silence linger. "I was too young to understand it all, but after my birth, she'd had difficulty carrying a child. That last time, I remember her excitement and her body getting larger...and then the babe was gone and she was in agony, confined to her bed."

His voice cracked and he set his cup down on the small table nearby before rubbing his palms over the fabric on his knees. "I used to sneak into her room to visit and tell her stories, trying to make her smile again."

"I'm sure she loved having you there."

"I think she did at first, but then something in her mind snapped. And a few days later, she slipped into a deep sleep and never woke up." He lifted his gaze to the elegant plasterwork on the ceiling as the rest of the story flowed out of the recesses where he had stuffed the memory.

"My father found me kneeling beside her cold body, crying and shaking her shoulders, begging God for her to awaken. He pulled me away from her and told me my behavior was a disgrace. That a future baron would never act that way."

"Surely his grief was speaking." Emma lifted shaking fingers to cover her mouth.

He shook his head. "Perhaps. But as a ten-year-old boy, I only wanted to please him. To make him proud. To not embarrass the Wentworth name. So at the funeral, I tried so hard to be honorable and stoic."

But his emotions had gotten the best of him. He'd been sent away from the church with Mrs. Richards and cried in her arms until there were no more tears to be shed. Yet another reason he needed to finish his business here to honor her legacy.

Moisture welled in Emma's eyes as if she could imagine the funeral scene. "You have to be true to yourself and your heart. There's no shame in loving well." She stretched across the small table and rested a hand on his forearm. "Oh, Wentworth. There's no doubt you loved your mother and she loved you."

Her softly-spoken words filled the gaping void that had grown during his years at Cambridge. For the first time since saying goodbye to the castle cook on the morning of his departure, his heart found comfort.

Emma's tears spilled over and trickled down her cheeks. Tears spent on his behalf from a heart already well acquainted with grief.

He twisted to face her, then gently wiped away the droplets. No doubt this woman was a treasure. "Thank you for understanding when others didn't." It was the least he could do to acknowledge her support.

But at the silky smoothness under his fingertips and the sea-foam shimmer in her eyes, he found himself wanting to give her so much more.

"Please, call me Grayson." In a motion that felt as natural as breathing, he leaned forward and brushed a kiss across her lips.

She drew in a quick breath, but did not pull away despite the questions in her eyes.

One kiss was not enough to express the depth of emotion building in his chest. But before he could lower his head for another taste, a murmur of voices filtered in through the drawing room door.

Voices that reminded him he was a mere visitor at Bainbridge Manor. The cold dash of reality had him shifting back into his chair and picking up his now-cold tea.

Personal feelings aside, he was supposed to be courting Emma's cousin.

Chapter Seven

Saturday evening, Emma set another platter of mutton on the dining room table, then hastily prepared a plate for herself as her cousin Julia exclaimed over her reception at her betrothed's home and the size of the Haddington library.

Leave it to Julia to be captivated by books while Cecilia had already described the Wexley music room in detail.

With a smile, Emma retreated to the far end of the table where she could keep an eye on the food and receive instructions from the kitchen without disturbing the others.

With the two traveling parties having arrived within an hour of each other, many of the household staff had been temporarily reassigned to assist with the unpacking of the assorted trunks, leaving Emma to help serve the meal as her aunt, uncle, and cousins dined.

As Emma ate, the conversation shifted from recapping the last few days—and Cecilia's official engagement—toward a timeline for announcements in the paper and even the plans for engagement parties and balls within the month.

"If my dressmaker is to prepare two complete wardrobes for the girls, we'll need to leave immediately for London so they can be fitted." Lady Rowley blotted her lips with a cloth napkin. "She may need to special order some of the fabrics and time is of the essence."

"I wish I could get away to accompany you, but there is unfinished business to be addressed here." Her uncle frowned.

His sister laughed. "Be honest. You abhor the frivolities of shopping, but your staff will be sufficient protection for the trip without you."

"How long will it take?" The baron took another serving of mutton.

"Even with a speedy carriage, it will still take over a week combined to get there and back. Not to mention we'll need at least a week or more in London." Lady Rowley glanced at her oldest two nieces.

The baron frowned, then raised his voice to be heard above the excitement an extended stay in London had aroused. "If you leave now, you won't be back to assist with or attend our Midsummer's Eve celebration."

"The villagers should understand our absence, and perhaps Phoebe could serve as hostess since she will be the eldest Miss Clarke in residence."

Emma winced. Technically, that role fell to her but reality favored only the daughters of the eldest son.

"Truly? Then can I wear mama's jewels, too?" Phoebe leaned forward eagerly but beside her, Julia burst into laughter.

Cecelia masked a smile behind a sip of wine. "Surely you won't let her do the planning?"

Her uncle chuckled. "Phoebe can grace the receiving line at my side in style, but I'll be sure to have Mrs. Carey see to the other arrangements."

Another task Emma was more than capable of overseeing. Would the rejection ever end?

"In the meantime, we've a trip to London to arrange."

"I have already written a friend who previously offered the use of her townhouse whenever I came to town."

The baron nodded. "That will save me some coin, but exactly how much is the rest of this trip going to cost?"

"Papa, we're only getting married once." Cecelia rolled her eyes and exchanged glances with Julia. "Then our husbands will assume financial responsibility. Surely you can afford to send us off in style."

"Will I be getting new gowns too?" Phoebe's question sparked more laughter and she stuck out her bottom lip. "I'll be in both weddings and I'm sure you wouldn't want me to be an embarrassment in an old gown."

Emma glanced down at her cast-off gown and the frayed fabric at her elbows. There would never be new fabric or dresses for her. Only hand-me-downs.

Eating around the lump in her throat was difficult, but did not halt her memory of the last time a Clarke offered to buy her fabric for a new dress.

That offer cost her aunt's life.

And on the evening of the funeral, she'd been called to her uncle's study and reminded of her status as the penniless orphan with no dowry. *You've cost me too much as it is, so from now on you'll be content with a roof over your head and food in your belly, or else I'll turn you out.*

His threat of expulsion had provided ample motivation to make herself indispensable in other ways while never forgetting her unwelcome place in the household.

If only there was a way to earn pocket money so she could buy her own clothes and not be so dependent on her uncle's strained hospitality.

From the other end of the table, she overheard a quote for a minimum wardrobe and swallowed her gasp. A mere fraction of that cost would pay a year's rent for a cottage in Danvers. Some things in life weren't fair.

With a heavy heart, Emma swallowed the last of her meal, then rose to clear the dishes and serve the next course to her relatives. Perhaps it would be easier on her heart to eat her meals with the servants instead.

Her uncle's booming voice caught her attention. "So, it's settled. You'll leave for London on Monday."

"If I wasn't getting to be the hostess for Midsummer's Eve, I'd be begging to go along now." Phoebe batted her eyelashes at her father. "But perhaps this fall—"

"Enough." His firm voice cut her pleading off and the sudden scowl on his face was enough to make Emma's blood run cold. "Young lady, I've been made aware of your behavior yesterday. Before you are allowed to go anywhere, we will come to an understanding where Lord Danvers is concerned."

Emma turned away and heat rose in her face at the memory of Grayson's kiss. Part of her rejoiced to see Phoebe squirm under the necessary reprimand while being equally relieved her uncle did not know the full story of how Emma had benefited from her cousin's absence.

She would treasure the memory of their private conversation for the rest of her life.

"There will be no more evasion from you." Her uncle slapped his hand onto the table top as if to emphasize his edict. "In fact, I sent a message to the vicarage inviting Lord Danvers to stay here for a few days and thoroughly expect him to arrive this evening."

Emma's heart clenched. Unless their other business was truly pressing, it seemed that a match was still possible between Phoebe and the handsome baron.

It would be wonderful to see him again from a distance, but she squirmed beneath the uncomfortable truth he'd soon be officially out of reach. And the sooner she accepted that fact, the better.

Phoebe burst into a tearful apology. "It was just a misunderstanding about what time he was calling and I wanted to go for a ride in the countryside instead. Why don't I get a say in my life and who I spend time with?"

Emma slipped out of the room with a tray piled with used dishes, happy to leave her immature cousin behind. After a few minutes gathering her composure, she returned to the dining room with their dessert.

Halfway through serving the fruit-topped cheesecake, there was an increase in noise near the entryway to the manor.

A moment later, Mr. Stafford entered the room. "My lord, Lord Danvers has arrived."

"Have his things taken to the blue room in the east wing, then tell him to join us for dessert." Her uncle waved a hand in Emma's direction. "Fetch another plate."

She had barely returned with another place setting when Grayson appeared in the doorway looking as handsome as ever. His eyes swept over the room lingering a bit on Phoebe—then her—and then back to her cousin before he strode forward to greet her uncle with a slight bow. "Thank you for your offer of hospitality."

Her uncle waved him toward a chair beside Phoebe, then motioned again for Emma to serve their guest.

Somehow, by the grace of God, she managed not to spill anything or otherwise reveal her sudden case of nerves over being close to him again.

While Grayson's arrival had triggered an uncomfortable silence in the room, he soon broke the tension by offering his sincere congratulations to both Cecilia and Julia on their engagements. Conversation naturally flowed from there into a resumed discussion of their wedding plans.

By the time Emma gathered the dessert plates, Grayson's presence was all but ignored. Until he cleared his throat. "If I might inquire—seeing as tomorrow is Sunday and I forgot to ask the vicar before I departed—what time are services?"

A stunned silence met his question.

He frowned. "Am I to assume I should make my own arrangements to travel to the church or—"

Her uncle's chuckle sounded forced. "You're welcome to join the family in our carriages." He cast a pointed glance at his sister and all three daughters.

Emma masked her smile by turning toward the kitchen. While Grayson was staying true to his faith convictions, his innocent questions had somewhat shamed her relatives into attending when they would normally have pleaded fatigue from their travels.

It would be good to see him at worship since it boded well for the future of Danvers, but her heart was torn. Especially since tomorrow she'd be attending the services with the servants.

Like always.

Separate from the rest of the family...and their guest.

Tuesday morning, Emma sought refuge in the kitchen.

How much longer until Grayson left for Danvers and she could regain her sanity?

It would be better if she could forget his invitation to call him by his Christian name and revert to a more formal address in her thoughts. And yet her heart refused to listen to reason, especially when her restless nights were filled with dreams featuring a certain baron who lived in a castle on the hill.

The longer the dreams continued, the harder her fantasies would crash on the inevitable rocks of reality. If only her mother hadn't filled her head with tales of King Arthur's knights.

Emma frowned as she sliced the last loaf of yesterday's bread into thick pieces for toast.

Despite her bedtime prayers, her heart refused to let go of hope that someday she'd escape Bainbridge Manor and return to her home by the sea. However, in reality, it was more likely that once her cousins married, her uncle would kick her out of his home, penniless and without position or prospects.

"What's got you so glum on such a fine day?"

Emma forced a smile as she turned to acknowledge the kindly cook who had let her invade the kitchen multiple times over the past two days.

"Does this have anything to do with our guest?" Mrs. Ashbrook's concerned face forced Emma to face the truth.

With a sigh, Emma set down the knife. "He's all the best my home has to offer."

"Your home?" The cook settled onto a stool beside the worktable. "You mean before you came to live here?"

Emma nodded. "I grew up in the village of Danvers just down the coast from King Arthur's castle. I lived under the shadow of the Wentworth Manor and the leadership of the former baron. I even played with Grayson, er, Wentworth...his lordship and the other children during the festivals before he was sent away to school." She inhaled a deep breath. "But despite my father being the second son of a baron, I have no claim to even an honorary title. Or a dowry. It's difficult to remember my childhood with one breath and still remember my proper place in society with the next."

"Making it uncomfortable to see that handsome young man everywhere you go in this house." Mrs. Ashbrook's gaze grew thoughtful as she darted a glance toward the place where Grayson had eaten his snack and then helped Emma make pastries almost a week before.

Emma clenched her jaw. "Foolish dreams aside, he will never be my future. But his presence has reminded me that I need to prepare for the day when all my cousins are married." She picked up the knife and began slicing again. "I can't stay here as an unpaid servant. I'm not opposed to honest work, but I require a fair wage."

A warm grip on her arm stilled her hand. "I had wondered how long it would be before you forced a change. Had he lived, your father would never have wished this life for you."

Emma turned to face her, begging for wisdom. "What am I to do?"

"I'll pray on your behalf. And perhaps I can help you think of a way to make some coin of your own so you can set some aside." The kind woman glanced around the room and even though they were alone, she lowered her voice. "I live in a cottage on the outskirts of Whitstone. If your situation gets desperate here, you are always welcome to stay with me."

Tears filled her eyes. There was a strong chance things could get dismal at best before she could break free. Still, despite the fairy tales her mother told, no knight in shining armor would be coming for her.

But perhaps God had sent a mothering cook instead.

Before she could accept the offer of shelter, one of the kitchen maids returned from the dairy and the time for private conversation had ended. Instead, Emma nodded, then turned her attention toward toasting the slices.

When it was time to carry a tray to the breakfast room, Mrs. Ashbrook nudged Emma through the door with a wink. "And eat a little something while you're there. God knows it's where you belong."

With shaking knees, Emma pushed into the room, then relaxed to find it empty. What had she been so afraid of?

But almost before she had prepared a plate for herself and taken a seat at the table, their house guest arrived.

His eyes fell upon her, then swept over the other empty chairs. "Are the others late risers or has Miss Phoebe's mysterious illness spread?"

Emma swallowed her quick retort and resorted to an unladylike shrug as she continued to eat. Oh, he deserved so much better than the lies he'd been told that kept him lingering at the manor.

After a quiet day of presumed private reflection on Sunday, the household had been in an uproar Monday as the Lady Rowley and the brides-to-be left for London. But even before they'd departed, her uncle had ridden toward Camelford to meet with a few business associates. It was a fact Phoebe had let slip while confiding that Mr. Smythe was going to approach him along the road and officially offer for her hand.

Emma risked a quick glance at Grayson as he gathered his own breakfast onto a small plate, then bowed his head in prayer.

In her father's absence yesterday, Phoebe had successfully feigned an illness to avoid being alone with Grayson. As a result, he had spent the day alone while Emma fought to guard her heart and not rush to keep him company.

Still, it hurt to see him first in the library reading a book—something she'd never been allowed to indulge in—and then to learn he'd ridden around the countryside by himself. She later heard that he'd spent time talking to the Whitstone villagers about farming techniques.

The Cornwall coastal soil might not be the richest, but it was possible to grow good things there. And his time had not been truly wasted if her home region would prosper as a result.

She finished her breakfast in awkward silence, then with a quick curtsy and whispered farewell, escaped down the hall back toward the kitchen.

Halfway there, Phoebe reached out and pulled her into an alcove. The sharp grip of her nails in Emma's arm mirrored the fierce whisper in her ear as she waved a folded piece of parchment in her face. "Francis is coming for me this morning, so you must help get me out of the house without Lord Danvers tagging along."

Emma stiffened. "I won't lie for you."

Her cousin glared. "You'll do as I say or else I'll have Papa kick you out so fast you'll wish you'd never interfered with my plans."

Empowered by Mrs. Ashbrook's offer of a temporary home, Emma stood her ground. "Our mothers were related, but my father grew up in this house. The previous baron was my grandfather, too." Phoebe gasped but the truth of Emma's identity wrapped around her heart. "What would your mother think to hear you say such things about your own flesh and blood?"

Phoebe shoved the note into her pocket, then stepped back folding her arms across her heaving chest. "Fine. I won't sneak out, but if you don't want me to tell Papa that you want Lord Danvers for yourself, you'd better get dressed to accompany me on the picnic I've just decided to arrange for the four of us."

Emma's pulse raced to have her secret hopes exposed so carelessly. Did Phoebe know or only suspect?

"Even if it means I have to be polite to Lord Danvers along the way, I won't let anything stand in the way of my seeing Francis today. Even you."

Emma's courage wavered and she nodded.

A moment later, Phoebe slipped away, leaving Emma scrambling to regain her composure.

Until she came up with a different plan for her survival, she needed to abide by Phoebe's wishes and maintain the peace. But could her heart survive another day in close proximity as the man of her dreams courted her cousin?

An hour after breakfast, Grayson found himself pacing the hallway outside the overwhelmingly blue bedchamber he'd been assigned in the east wing.

Miss Phoebe had sent word for him to be ready in a half hour for an outdoor picnic. Other than their first pairing during the dinner party and a crowded walk in the gardens, she had expertly—or purposeful-ly—avoided being alone with him.

Meaning today could be his only chance to discover her character and capture her attention.

That thought led to another from a different conversation where her cousin had revealed Miss Phoebe's affinity for gifts.

Yesterday while touring the countryside around Whitstone, he'd been tempted to spend money he couldn't afford on a small trinket as a token of his intentions, but after nearly running into Mrs. Pembroke and the equally inquisitive innkeeper's wife outside the village warehouse, he had changed his mind.

What was it Mrs. Richards used to say? That love and truth mattered more than the trappings of wealth and position. And Emma had said something similar a few days ago...that he had to be true to his own heart first.

If he bowed to the pressure of his peers, would he remain true to his identity as a child of God and a leader of men? Even if it was only over a small village of miners and fishermen with a harbor badly in need of repair, if he didn't respect himself, he couldn't expect others to do the same.

Starting with his future wife.

Would she respect their need to exercise frugality for a season? If Miss Phoebe was destined to be that woman, could she ever submit her will to the restrictions of their accounts?

Grayson checked the clock on a nearby table. Soon he would have the opportunity to discover the truth.

If only loyalty to his father's memory hadn't overridden his common sense. He never should have added his own signature to the betrothal contract.

Perhaps Lord Bainbridge would accept the withdrawal of his offer like a gentleman. After all, they still had another item of unfinished business to discuss. Except over the past two days, the man had been as absent as his supposedly-ailing daughter.

Even Emma had been scarce, although he'd seen her here and there, usually wearing an apron as though she were a servant in the household and not a relative. After Friday's tea—and kiss—in the drawing room, he couldn't stop thinking about her. But following her lead to keep his distance was wise for both their sakes.

He pounded a fist into the palm of his other hand. If he could just finalize the details today, he could be home by tomorrow night albeit with a much lighter purse.

After bestowing the final bequest, there would be precious little to live on until the fall harvest. And without an additional dowry, there would be no margin for error, but plenty of work to keep his mind and body occupied. He would have to trust God to provide.

After another glance at the clock, he proceeded down the stairs to finish waiting there while perusing the family portraits in the gallery outside the drawing room.

The sooner this outing began, the sooner he would have his answers. And if Miss Phoebe left him stranded again, he would force the issue with her father and be free by nightfall.

A few minutes later, noise by the main door caught his attention and he turned in time to see a footman showing Mr. Smythe into the entryway.

Dread settled in his stomach at the prospect of another awkward encounter. He would rather cede the victory to the other man and bow out gracefully than uphold the appearance of a competition for Miss Phoebe's hand.

However, before he could greet Mr. Smythe, he heard soft feminine voices descending the stairs and turned to watch the arrival of the lavishly-attired debutante with a subdued Emma trailing three steps behind her.

Standing near the foot of the stairs, he caught Miss Phoebe's glance at Mr. Smythe and the slight shake of her head. The other man clenched his fists as he stepped back.

What was that about?

"Lord Danvers." Miss Phoebe bypassed her preferred beau to greet him with a deep curtsy before clutching his arm possessively. "I'm so looking forward to our picnic today."

As if avoiding him yesterday had been a mistake? Why the sudden change in behavior?

Out of the corner of his eye, he spied the baron peeking around the corner near his study and his stomach cramped at the realization her actions were all for show.

Before he could shake the liar off his arm, Mr. Smythe grunted, then pushed forward to greet Emma with an exaggerated bow of his own. The man then clasped her hand and despite Emma's obvious discomfort over the unwelcome attention, made a show of kissing the backs of her fingers while gushing his admiration for the unique color of her eyes.

Grayson's protective instincts welled up with the desire to pull Emma away. No, not simply protective, but also jealous. Yet he had no right to feel jealousy while practically engaged to her cousin. Still, no woman deserved to be treated thus.

Emma turned to her cousin and the betrayal in her eyes first froze him in place...then drove him to action. He would make this outing safe for her and somehow bring a smile back to her face. She deserved that and so much more.

He tugged Miss Phoebe closer to the other couple, forcing Mr. Smythe to step back or get his toes trampled. "Just where are we headed today?"

"I've arranged for a carriage ride to take us to the perfect spot for a picnic. It's down the river near the village church." Miss Phoebe glanced over her shoulder. Her father must not have been watching any longer, for she suddenly released his arm and stepped toward Mr. Smythe.

Chapter Eight

The open carriage swayed as their driver took his place on the high perch behind Emma and after a snap of the reins, they lurched into motion, the wooden wheels clattering over the cobblestones drive.

Emma braced her feet and fought to maintain her distance from the odious Mr. Smythe seated beside her on the narrow rear-facing bench.

Her skin still crawled with the memory of his moist lips on her fingers...and his subsequent bold declaration they should get better acquainted. The overblown gesture had done nothing to change her impression of him as a self-absorbed dandy. Especially when his eyes had been on Phoebe the entire time.

Other than his obvious wealth, what did her cousin see in the man?

Riding while facing backward sometimes gave her a queasy stomach, but today it also gave her an unobstructed view of Grayson's strong features, made only more distinct with his dark hair pulled back from his forehead.

Her fingers twitched with the urge to loosen the ribbon at his nape and see if the strands still held the wave she remembered from their childhood.

With heat rising in her cheeks, she diverted her gaze over his shoulder at the receding view of Bainbridge Manor, but her rebellious thoughts recalled their personal conversation over tea on Friday before he bestowed her first kiss. A kiss delivered with both compassion and warmth in his blue eyes.

Not fifteen minutes ago, those same eyes had held an icy fury at Mr. Smythe's actions as if like one of King Arthur's knights, he'd wanted to defend Emma's honor.

But despite her foolish daydreams, Grayson's title required that he seek a wife with a proper heritage and a substantial dowry. She simply had to accept the reality that he was out of reach.

And unless God worked a miracle, Emma would be alone and vulnerable to unwelcome advances like Mr. Smythe's for the rest of her life.

As the carriage wheels turned off the cobblestone driveway onto a dirt path leading toward the river, Phoebe's chatter suddenly filled the previous silence.

While her cousin loved to hear herself talk, something about her overly-bright tone raised Emma's suspicions and drew her attention to her cousin's flushed face. Because while Phoebe's effusion of words about the history of the area and breadth of the manor property were obviously directed toward the newcomer Grayson, her heated gaze never left Mr. Smythe.

Out of the corner of her eye, Emma checked for Mr. Smythe's reaction, only to find him staring at Phoebe with something akin to resolve. Followed by a subtle twitch of his head toward the river.

Phoebe nodded, then after a quick glance upward to where the driver perched, turned her attention to Grayson as her vivacious monologue continued.

Emma narrowed her eyes. Obviously she had missed something important in the exchange, because based on Phoebe's earlier words in the alcove, her cousin had no true desire to spend time with Grayson today. Which meant that like a player in a theatrical production, Phoebe's feigned interest in the visiting baron—and Mr. Smythe's earlier unwelcome attentions—were for the benefit of her father and his eavesdropping—and possibly tattling—employee alone.

And despite her cousin's threat to unveil Emma's interest in the young baron, Phoebe might yet expect her to occupy their house guest's attention so she could carry on her own flirtation without consequence.

Trying to separate the truth from the drama only made Emma's head ache. Oh, why had she let her cousin talk her into this outing?

Emma turned away from the other occupants of the carriage to study the sprawling countryside as they neared the river.

Even if it was a beautiful day for a drive through the very land her father had once roamed, she'd give anything for an ocean view instead.

God, help me find a way to break free of the family obligations that keep me chained here.

At nineteen, she was old enough to marry, except she'd likely need her guardian's permission to do so. Or she could wait another year and a half in service elsewhere until she was fully of age and in control of her own destiny.

Forgive me, God. You alone are in control. But if there is a way to return home and experience the love of a happy family again, let it be so.

A cleared throat nearby caught her attention and she turned to find Grayson waiting with an outstretched hand to assist her down from the stopped carriage while behind him, Phoebe stood next to Mr. Smythe.

Emma's eyes widened and heat spread across her face. "Oh, my goodness." Rising quickly, she put her fingers in his for support and with a pounding heart at the warm contact, maneuvered her wide skirts through the narrow opening in the side of the carriage.

"Percy, once you've unloaded and set up our picnic, you can drive on to the village to pick up the things on this list. We'll look for your return in two hours." Phoebe's sharp voice dismissing the coachman pierced through the fog of Emma's distraction.

Emma paused on the top step in shock. "But that would—"

Phoebe cut her off with a glare as she handed a folded piece of parchment to the frowning servant. "Emma's presence will be adequate as chaperone." She turned to Mr. Smythe and tilted her head. "Perhaps you would be so kind as to assist so he can be on his way?"

As if the sooner they could rid themselves of the not-so-impartial observer and drop the acting, the better.

"Of course." Mr. Smythe stepped to the rear of the carriage, plucking the basket from the protesting coachman's grasp before striding toward the tree line.

Slight pressure on her fingers brought Emma back to the present and the realization that she still stood on the top step of the carriage with her hand in Grayson's.

"Oh, I've done it again." She grasped her skirts with her free hand and descended.

"A penny for your thoughts?" Grayson's eyes held a hint of humor that mirrored the teasing angle of his smile.

Emma's heart pounded in response to his words and courteous touch, but once her feet were on the ground, she tugged her hand free. "I'm not sure they're worth that much."

Phoebe snorted, then took Grayson's arm, steering him toward the river. "It's a lovely day for a picnic."

The two soon discussed the weather as they strolled toward where the coachman spread several blankets in the shade beneath the trees.

Emma swallowed her disappointment at being brushed aside and trailed after the courting couple. Once again, not a servant but not a daughter or guest either. A nobody.

Underfoot, a slightly worn path in the grass reminded her that the footbridge leading to the village lay nearby, but out of sight around a few trees. Did Mrs. Ashbrook travel this way to and from the manor? It wouldn't be too far to walk.

However, if Emma was forced to seek shelter with the kindly cook, it was unlikely she'd be allowed employment within the manor walls. Meaning the cook's offer could only be a temporary solution.

God, show me what to do. Make my future path straight.

Once they reached the picnic location, Grayson assisted Phoebe to a seated position on the blankets. Emma ignored Mr. Smythe's clammy hand and instead sank to her knees beside the picnic basket.

With the coachman's firm command to the horses echoing behind her, she reached into the depths of the basket that contained their luncheon.

"I'm not at all hungry." Phoebe had retrieved a fan from her hidden pocket and tapped it against her skirts.

Emma paused and drew in a steadying breath. "Perhaps a snack then? Mrs. Ashbrook packed a bowl of fresh berries."

Her cousin huffed. "How provincial."

Situated between them, Grayson reached for a sample and popped it into his mouth. "Berries always remind me of Midsummer's Eve. It is one of my favorite celebrations."

Emma's smile returned with the memories of home and her mother's baking. "Mine too." She fingered her mother's locket.

"You would think so." Phoebe sneered. "Personally, I find the old traditions boring."

Mr. Smythe leaned forward and lowered his voice. "You, my dear Miss Clarke, are never boring."

Phoebe giggled and batted her eyes at him over the top of her open fan.

Emma resisted the urge to roll her eyes and guided the conversation back to include their house guest. "Lord Bainbridge hosts a party in the manor ballroom like his ancestors before him, but I think Midsummer's Eve is meant to be spent out of doors like it was when I was a child."

Phoebe frowned as if she resented Emma's intrusion on the conversation. "Our celebration might seem like just another party to you, but I personally prefer to avoid all those bugs and the heat."

With a deliberate lift of her chin, Emma held her ground. "Maybe it's better outdoors if you're by the sea with the breeze coming off the water, but my favorite memories are when the baron's family invited us up to their castle on the cliff and mixed with the villagers for a day of games and music and food."

"A castle on the cliff?" Grayson raised an eyebrow. "That sounds very much like it could be my estate, although ours aren't the only rocky cliffs along the coast."

Mr. Smythe coughed to cover his laugh and Emma grimaced.

She'd heard that smugglers counted on the region's cliffs to cause shipwrecks, but also carved out caves as hiding places for their loot. Loot that if rumor were true made its way inland through channels controlled by Mr. Smythe's family. At a profit that may have paid for the expensive fabric of his jacket.

Emma turned her back on the scoundrel and faced Grayson instead. "Surely you know that your people call Wentworth Manor the castle on the cliff."

"They do." He frowned as if trying to figure something out. "But how would you know that?"

Phoebe snorted, then reached a hand to the man on her right. "Mr. Smythe, will you accompany me on a stroll? There are other things I'd rather do on such a lovely day than listen to Emma talk about her precious cliffs. Dumb rocks hold no fascination for me."

Emma winced at the familiar slight, but as her cousin wandered off into the trees, she embraced the temporary freedom to be herself.

"She's heard me talk of home too many times, but those particular cliffs hold a lot of memories." She waved a hand toward the scar on Grayson's puzzled face. "Even if it can be quite dangerous on the edge of the cliff."

He rubbed a hand over the spot. "How did you know?"

She smiled at the poignant memory. "I was there."

Grayson's fingertips traced the indentation on his cheek. "You were there? How is that possible?" The accident had happened ten years before, when he was twelve.

Lines creased Emma's forehead, then eased as her smile grew. "I know I mentioned that I grew up along the coast, but I suppose I never actually said it was in Danvers."

"Danvers." His home.

He scrambled to recall their past conversations and how old she was when she'd moved away from the coast. No wonder she knew about the mine accident and had asked about the villagers.

Faint feminine laughter floated on the breeze. He should care that Miss Phoebe had wandered off unchaperoned with Mr. Smythe, but a conversation with Emma was so much more interesting. And beneficial.

Since she knew the Danvers area personally, Emma could let him know how his continued plans for improvements would be received. While the villagers deferred to his title, because of his age, he still needed to earn their respect.

But where to start? With the harbor or the mine?

"I still remember that day when Tobias's little brother got too close to the edge and fell." Emma's sweet voice drew him into the past.

"Ah, Tobias Hadley." The annual celebrations were the only time his father hadn't frowned upon Grayson's mingling with the village children. Of course, that hadn't stopped him from sneaking off with his best friend whenever he could. "We couldn't go anywhere without Andrew trailing behind, but I hadn't thought he'd follow us there."

Grayson flinched at the memories of his friend's panic and the terror-filled cries rising up from below. "But once he fell, we couldn't wait for someone to get help, and since I was the strongest, I was nominated to—"

"You volunteered to stretch down over the edge and pull him up." Emma's eyes glowed with admiration.

His chest swelled at the recognition of his intended heroics, then reality intruded and he brushed aside the undeserved attention with a self-conscious chuckle. "But I didn't count on the fact Tobias and the other boys might not be strong enough to lift us both back up."

"We girls helped too, but you still smashed into the rocks." Her gaze dipped again to his cheek.

Grayson winced at the memory of dangling over the edge and being unable to protect his face from the jagged surface. "But I never let go of little Andrew."

The teary look of joy on the boy's face to be rescued had made the pain worth it. And that was before Grayson had turned to face the circle of applauding children.

Emma giggled. "And then Tobias fainted at the sight of the blood running down your cheek."

"I still remember there was a girl who gave me her handkerchief to press against the cut. Once the village men arrived, I never got the chance to thank her properly."

A rosy blush bloomed on her cheeks. "You're welcome."

It was Emma's handkerchief? His smile grew. "No wonder you knew all about it. Injury aside, it was a memorable Midsummer's Eve celebration that year." He laughed, then sobered. "I hadn't realized it would be my last one before being sent off to school."

Emma shifted on the picnic blanket and stared off into the trees. "Why didn't you come home over the summers? Surely you had time off from your studies."

He sighed. "My father arranged for me to spend my breaks visiting other estates to continue my education." And mingle with more noble families in hopes of growing their connections. Except the only place he'd longed for had been home.

Grayson stretched out his legs. "Since my father died, I've been busy with the estate accounts and sea wall repairs so I haven't been able to visit everyone in the area. Whatever happened to Tobias and Andrew?"

When Emma turned back to face him, a sheen of tears in her eyes. "The small pox hit the village hard."

Right. Her mother had died from the disease after caring for others. Did that mean—?

"The Hadley boys survived with scars but lost both of their parents and one young sister. I heard that Tobias hired out to a farm near Boscastle while Andrew stayed home to care for their surviving siblings."

He nodded. More children he might be guardian for. "When I return to Danvers, I'll be sure to check on them." And all of the others too.

She smiled. "I knew you'd grow up to be the kind of leader who truly cares about the people."

"Can you keep a secret?"

She nodded and he leaned forward. "After my mother died, I used to wish I lived in the village."

"It must have been lonely up there on the hill." Sympathy shone in her eyes.

He cleared his throat. "It was. Except for..."

"For what?"

"Actually, my favorite memory during those years was spending time with our cook. She was like a mother to me. She even let me help sometimes. And for special occasions, she baked a variation of those fruit pastries you made except there would be a toy or note inside."

"I'll have to bake you one of her party pockets."

"How would you...?" He blinked at the new realization. Since Emma was from Danvers, she might know where to find—

"She experimented at home with new recipes before taking them up to the manor house."

His breath caught in his throat. "You're Miss Richards? I thought you were a Miss Clarke. The baron's niece and granddaughter of the previous baron." He waved a hand back toward the manor house while scrambling to retrace their introductions...and her cousin's insistence on calling her *just Emma*. As if she were a nobody. A commoner. A servant. When instead she was...

The lovely woman shrugged her slim shoulders. "Legally, I'm a Clarke because of my father, but in my heart, my mother's second husband, Mr. Richards, was more of a father than I deserved." She fingered the tin locket around her neck.

The same locket he'd seen so many times before around the neck of their cook Mrs. Richards. No wonder he'd felt so treasured and understood during his conversations with Emma.

"You truly are just like your mother in all the best ways."

Her eyes shone with gratitude as she dropped her voice to a whisper. "Thank you."

The pressure in his chest grew with love for their cook and a reminder of the other reason he'd come to the Whitstone area. His second task to track down her surviving descendant had been virtually accomplished without Lord Bainbridge's assistance after all.

And to think that Mrs. Richard's bright-eyed daughter—the object of his first real infatuation as a boy—had grown up into a quiet beauty with intriguing sea-foam green eyes. A woman who now knew all the intricacies of societal etiquette but lived as a servant when she didn't need to anymore.

"Your mother would be so proud of the woman you've become." He shifted closer to Emma.

She caught her breath and looked down at her folded hands in her lap. No. She had to accept the truth.

With gentle fingers, Grayson lifted her face until he had captured her gaze. "Truly. You have no idea how glad I am to have found you again."

Her pink lips opened in surprise and a flash of attraction jolted his heart. It was the same sensation he'd tried to forget after Friday's unchaperoned conversation in the library. But his new knowledge of her identity left him unable to resist her allure and he lowered his mouth to cover hers.

After a quick gasp, she leaned into their connection and his fingers moved from her chin to cradle her face. One kiss melded into another until he could almost taste the sweet pastries on her lips as she returned his kisses.

When her slim hands clutched the fabric of his shirt, he realized his heart beat wildly in his chest. They had crossed into a dangerous zone and reluctantly he eased away, pressing her head to rest against the fabric of his jacket as he fought to catch his breath.

And fully embraced the overwhelming sensation of coming home with her in his arms.

To have grown up together and then found each other again when he was in the position of seeking a wife.

If only he could win her heart instead.

Make Emma his wife.

"I wish you could be mine."

She gasped and straightened, staring at him with bright emotion in her eyes. Was that hope?

A smile stretched his face as resolve settled around his heart. And with it came the long-absent peace he'd sought since talking to her uncle about the betrothal contract almost a week before.

"As soon as we return to the manor, I'll arrange an audience with your uncle and retract my offer for Phoebe. That alliance was something my father wanted years ago, but it will never work."

"Truly? But..." A hint of insecurity clouded her eyes before she glanced down at her worn gown.

Once again, he lifted her chin until she gazed into his eyes. "Danvers needs *you*. *I* need you."

He sealed his declaration with a quick kiss, then rested his forehead against hers. "Thank You, Lord, for bringing us together."

"Amen." Emma's whispered words held the same mixture of awe and determination that pounded in his chest.

A burst of Phoebe's laughter from the nearby woods had them jumping apart. As Emma busied herself setting out food items from the basket, Grayson stood and wandered across the clearing as if merely stretching his legs.

All the while, waves of joy washed away his earlier worries about finding the right wife.

He'd sort out the financial implications later.

Chapter Nine

A fter an exhausting picnic lunch spent pretending interest in Phoebe's rambling chatter while attempting to ignore both her blatant flirtations with Mr. Smythe and Emma's shy glances, Grayson had never been so glad to return to Bainbridge Manor.

Once inside, he excused himself from the ladies and hurried to his room to retrieve his packet of papers. The sooner he could speak to the baron, the sooner he would be free to officially pursue the woman who had completely captured his heart.

Between a girlish handkerchief and a platter of apple pastries, Emma had shown her care in the most practical of ways.

And in return he could give her a home by the sea.

With barely veiled restraint, he descended the stairs. Now, where to find the baron at this hour?

As if orchestrated by God, the man stepped out of his study.

"My lord, can you spare a few moments?"

The baron raised an eyebrow, and a gleam appeared in his eyes. "Certainly." He gestured for Grayson to follow him back inside. "Finally got her to come around, did you?"

"Her?" Grayson blinked, then remembered the man's unattached daughter Phoebe. "Actually, during our limited time together, I realized that we will never—"

"You will never be happy without her by your side? Congratulations, my boy."

Grayson's spine stiffened at the man's demeaning tone.

"Any man with your perseverance and integrity will do fine by my girl." Lord Bainbridge took his seat behind his desk and unlocked the top drawer.

Grayson remained standing, bracing his resolve as the other man pulled out the already-prepared betrothal contract. "Things have changed and I need to—"

"No need." The baron waved a dismissive hand and reached for his pen. "Your father would be happy to see the day our families unite."

The mention of his father brought with it the weighty responsibility to maintain his integrity at all costs and do nothing to sully the Wentworth name. But nothing on the contract necessarily needed to change other than the bride's name.

Before Grayson could clarify his intentions, Lord Bainbridge scrawled the wrong name across the first blank line.

Grayson gasped. "Wait."

The other man merely raised an eyebrow, then dipped his pen again, preparing to sign the bottom of the document. A visibly altered document that now held additional scribbling in the margins.

"Stop this instant." Grayson slammed a hand down onto the desktop and pulled the papers closer so he could read the scrawling handwriting.

As the words sunk in, blood pounded in his forehead and his hands clenched in fury. The greedy baron had designated a modest dowry for his youngest daughter but then added a clause to the contract stipulating that if either party broke the terms, the offending party would not only repay or return any settlements immediately but also forfeit an additional sum as a penalty.

A significant sum that would bankrupt the Danvers estate for years to come and spell the demise of the title that had been in his family for generations.

Why add such a clause? Unless Lord Bainbridge already knew of his precarious financial situation and now used it to trap Grayson into an unwanted marriage.

Grayson's vision blurred as the blood drained from his head. "I would never agree to that."

Lord Bainbridge smirked as he tapped the bottom of the page. "You already have. That's your signature, isn't it? And once I finally add my signature, this contract is binding and will hold up in any court of law."

Grayson sucked in a quick breath. His rash actions signing the contract in defense of his father's name had also signed away his future.

Danvers had suffered enough. Which meant he would be required to honor his word, even if his heart was broken in the process.

"Unless..." The baron drew out the word as if baiting a hook.

Even knowing that it never turned out well for the fish, Grayson still bit on the hope it contained. "Unless what?"

God, please let there be a way out of this disaster.

"How badly do you wish for me to reject this contract?" The baron's eyes held a shrewd gleam that raised Grayson's level of caution. "I might be willing to tear up this document if we can reach a different agreement."

Grayson sank onto a chair and pressed his hands on his knees. Did he really want to know? "What sort of agreement?"

Over the next few minutes, the baron described a hypothetical arrangement where Grayson would use his authority along the coast to the benefit of a smuggling network in exchange for a substantial financial boon.

He would never have to worry about his bank balance again and would be free to marry the woman of his personal choice.

But turning a blind eye to illegal activity went against everything he believed and accepting a bribe in any form would put him on the same level as the lawbreakers. Not to mention, agreeing to the baron's sickening proposal would openly invite an unsavory element to taint his beloved village more than smuggling already had.

"What will it be?" The man waved a fleshy hand at the betrothal document before him and reached for the pen. "Marriage...or money?"

The cost was too high. Life with Phoebe would be difficult, but he'd never be able to live with himself if he accepted the man's vile offer.

He shook his head. "You know I cannot agree to—"

"Your loss." With a false smile, Lord Bainbridge signed the contract with a flourish.

Slamming the bars of an iron cage around Grayson's heart.

Making Grayson wish he could strike back somehow. "Will you be adding the date too?"

The other man smirked. "If you insist." With another slash of the pen he added both the date and time to the bottom of the contract, then initialed and dated the addendum as well.

The man returned his pen to its holder and leaned back in his chair, settling his hands across his wide girth. "Satisfied?"

Not even close, but he had only himself to blame.

With a heavy heart, Grayson took the parchment as if for a closer look, then folded it and placed it in his pocket. "I'll be keeping this lest you decide to add anything else."

The baron's eyes narrowed. "We could have worked well together. However, if I know my daughter, Phoebe's tastes will have you seeing the need for more income before the year is out. Family notwithstanding, when you eventually come crawling back for help, I may not be in as generous a mood. A pity that you missed your chance."

He'd missed his chance at happiness too.

The sudden vision of the joy in Emma's green eyes reminded him that his wasn't the only broken heart left in the wake of the baron's actions.

How would he face her again after their kisses? After his romantic declarations? His stomach churned at the thought of causing her pain. Of seeing the betrayal in her eyes.

Even if he could explain his actions, she'd still be alone at the end of the day. And there was nothing he could do...

No. There was something.

He might be trapped by his word and the document in his pocket, but at least he could set Emma free from her uncle's influence.

Set her free to find love somewhere else. He could give her a home even if he couldn't give her his heart or his name.

Grayson cleared his throat. "You may consider this settled, but there is another matter I had wished to speak to you about."

With more joy than she'd ever experienced within the walls of Bainbridge Manor, Emma twirled around her modest bedroom at the far end of the family's wing as if she were a debutante dancing at her first ball.

Hands holding her outstretched skirts, she dipped into a regal curtsy...then giggled as she rose.

Lord Danvers—her beloved Grayson—wanted her to be his wife. Had said he needed her. Had never forgotten about her.

She pressed a trembling hand over her pounding heart. The heroic boy from her childhood had grown into a handsome man...and like the romantic tales that permeated her dreams, the humble daughter of the castle cook might truly become the next baroness.

If only her mother were still alive to see the day. And what would her father think?

A brisk knock on the door brought her back to the present and she crossed quickly to answer the summons.

Mr. Stafford paused at the threshold with an odd look on his face. "Emma...Miss Clarke...Lord Bainbridge and Lord Danvers have requested an audience in your uncle's study."

Emma nodded. "I'll be along directly."

After the man left, she turned to the small mirror on her wall to check her hair, then with a growing smile, smoothed her dress over her fluttering midsection.

Her future was about to change forever.

A minute later, she descended the main stairs and prepared to face her uncle. Despite the memory of their kisses and the whispered prayer that bound her heart to Grayson's, her uncle would not be happy to have his niece chosen above his own daughter.

His moods were unpredictable at best. But God willing, soon she would be freed from his authority.

Approaching the closed door, Emma nodded for the butler to announce her arrival, then a moment later stepped into her uncle's private domain.

As expected, the frowning baron sat behind his massive desk, but Grayson stood gazing out the windows with his back to her. She'd been announced, so why wouldn't he make eye contact?

Stopping a few feet from her uncle, Emma dropped into the expected curtsy. "You sent for me, my lord?"

"Actually, young Wentworth wished to speak with you about something." Her uncle cast a quick glance at the younger baron.

Out of the corner of her eye, she saw Grayson stiffen at the deliberate slight but he still didn't turn.

Why would her uncle ignore his title as an equal peer in the realm? And why didn't he defend himself?

Emma's stomach roiled with the growing realization that something was amiss.

Her uncle cleared his throat. "But since he's already betrothed—"

"Betrothed?" Already? Based on Grayson's actions earlier, that didn't make any sense. Emma shook off her confusion and stared at the stern man behind the desk.

"Betrothed." His lips lifted into the ghost of a satisfied smile. "Until he presented his father's documents last week, I had almost forgotten about our bargain."

Last week? Before Grayson arrived at the manor or on the day of the dinner party when he'd asked to see her uncle? Surely circumstances had changed since then.

And yet as the paintings on the dark paneled walls blurred on the fringes of her vision, her dreams of a happy future also began to fade.

"...just signed the contract this afternoon." Lord Bainbridge leaned back in his chair and laced his fingers atop his chest.

What had she missed? Who signed? Grayson or her uncle? But no matter, if it was signed, the marriage was as good as sealed in the eyes of God.

Was there yet some chance of her name upon the agreement?

"You're the first to hear of Phoebe's good fortune."

Emma swallowed the rush of bile and her disappointment, struggling to keep her emotions from her face as her uncle shot another glance at the silent man beside the windows.

"Since you're originally from the coast, you can advise your cousin as she prepares to become the next Lady Danvers."

With braced feet to keep from swaying, Emma faced the painful truth. Despite their emotional connection and shared history, Grayson had chosen to marry her cousin.

And she'd been foolish to ever believe she could have captured his heart.

If only she could escape somewhere private to grieve the loss of her dreams and make alternate plans for her lonely future.

"Like I said, with Wentworth already betrothed to my daughter, for the sake of social propriety, I cannot grant you a private audience..."

Right. The true reason she'd been summoned in the first place delivered with a not-so-subtle jab at her common upbringing and the integrity of the man who finally turned from the window with a bleak expression.

His eyes seemed more gray than blue as they practically begged for her forgiveness. He'd vowed to speak to her uncle and withdraw his offer and the deep lines creasing his forehead made it clear that the outcome of their meeting had not been of his choosing.

As difficult as it would be to remain single, how perfectly horrid for him to marry a woman he did not love.

Despite her breaking heart, Emma lifted her chin and retreated behind the facade of proper manners drilled into her by her aunt. "May I offer my congratulations, my lord."

Grayson—Lord Danvers—briefly closed his eyes and a vein ticked along his jawline as he swallowed hard.

"Let's get on with it." Her uncle slapped his hand upon his desk. "I haven't all day."

Lord Danvers pulled a packet of folded documents from the inside pocket of his jacket and stepped closer as he unfolded them. He took a deep breath and stared over her shoulder. "My father's will left bequests to certain of his servants and their families. It took me this long to track the last one down."

His gaze shifted to hers. "As you already know, I didn't fully realize who you were until earlier today. But you are the beneficiary I was seeking."

She caught her breath. "The what?"

"Her?" Her uncle's outburst echoed her own disbelief. "That isn't possible."

"First, here is the deed declaring you, Emma Richards, the owner of a cottage in Danvers."

"A cottage? Truly?" For the first time since learning of her cousin's betrothal, hope began to grow. She would not have to remain under her uncle's roof forever.

Lord Danvers handed the first document to her and glanced at the next page. "You are also the recipient of an annual income of one hundred pounds."

Her uncle's gasp echoed her own. While a pittance by the baron's standards, it was more than enough to support her for life with enough left to hire a general housemaid if she wished.

"Once you are settled, this banknote will serve to transfer this year's funds at your discretion."

A home of her own and an income? By the sea? It was a dream of a different sort.

"You fool."

At her uncle's harsh words, Emma turned to find him staring at Lord Danvers with wide eyes. "That's throwing away money. She never had to know, especially when she already has a place here."

A place of perpetual servitude without pay. But never a place of belonging as a true family member, especially when her own flesh and blood would easily deny her a rightful inheritance.

Tears misted Emma's vision as she reached out to accept the second document and her ticket to freedom. "Thank you."

"Don't you even dare think about leaving until after the weddings. Your cousins need you."

The weight of family obligations settled upon her shoulders. Should she stay for another year or not? Was she truly needed at Bainbridge Manor?

No. Other maids could easily complete the necessary tasks.

"If you'll excuse me, I have much to consider." With a noncommittal nod at her uncle and a half-smile at the younger baron, Emma held onto her composure until she had exited the study.

Halfway up the stairs, her volatile emotions caught up with her and she dashed the rest of the way to her room where sobs shook her body as she collapsed onto her bed.

Grayson would be marrying her cousin and soon Phoebe—not Emma—would live in the castle as his wife. Meanwhile, thanks to the deceased baron, Emma had her forever home by the sea...alone.

To be in the shadow of her dream but denied the blessing of love was cruel.

But as hard as it would be to live that close to the man she loved, being a bystander to her cousin's wedding preparations would be even worse.

Especially when she wasn't truly needed.

A shriek of outrage echoed down the hall from the direction of Phoebe's room. Because of Emma's inheritance? Or more likely because she had learned of her engagement to Lord Danvers when she obviously preferred the dandified Mr. Smythe.

Dreading the inevitable summons to her cousin's side, Emma sat up and wiped the tears from her face.

Her eyes fell upon the inked parchment she'd been given. She did not have to stay within these walls and endure her cousin's drama when she'd been offered freedom instead.

The freedom to live among the friends from her childhood. Freedom to fill her days as she wished, even if that meant baking her mother's recipes and selling the goods to the villagers or Wentworth Manor.

And with her inheritance as a dowry, she even had the freedom to find a husband to love.

Or not.

But at least it would be her choice to make.

Emma opened the trunk at the foot of her bed, then crossed to her wardrobe for an armful of worn gowns.

Her future—lonely as it might be—started now.

Chapter Ten

G rayson entered his room with a slow tread and a heavy heart. Was it just this morning when he'd paced the hall debating his future? A future now set and sealed with the horrid document in his pocket.

He had tried to be honorable to his father's wishes and his personal word, but somehow the entire quest had left his heart bruised beyond repair.

But at least he still had his integrity. Under no circumstances could he have accepted a bribe of profits and turned a blind eye to the smugglers infecting the region. Honoring God came before pleasing men.

Even if it doomed him to a life of loneliness.

With resolve, he crossed to the wardrobe and tucked the depressing document safely away at the bottom of his bag. As he moved a folded jacket to cover the evidence of his foolishness, his fingers brushed the strand of his mother's pearls and he pulled them out.

The heirloom was the only tangible gift he had to give to his future bride. Would she accept them in the spirit they were intended or wrinkle her nose in disgust?

Grayson's shoulders slumped. Soon, he would know the answer, for Lord Bainbridge had promised to tell his daughter about the betrothal, then made plans for them all to meet in the drawing room in a half hour's time for a celebratory tea. Once the gift was delivered, Grayson would be free to leave in the morning.

A knock at the door pulled him from his plans, but as he turned, he caught a glimpse of himself in the mirror. He forced a smile but feared he would never truly be happy again.

If only the bride was Emma.

Grayson opened the door to the sight of a young footman shifting nervously on his feet.

The servant raised his voice to be heard above the high-pitched scream filtering down the hall from the family's rooms. "My Lord Bainbridge sends his apologies, but your meeting over tea must be postponed."

Grayson's shoulders relaxed at the reprieve, but at the sound of a loud crash, he peered down the carpeted hall. "Is someone in need?"

The footman winced, but did not appear otherwise concerned. "No need to concern yourself, m'lord. She'll calm down soon enough."

She. Phoebe. His future bride.

Grayson's stomach cramped and his appetite fled. If her reaction to the news of their marriage had canceled tea, what would the evening meal entail?

"Should I have a tray sent up instead?" The footman raised an eyebrow as if guessing the direction of his thoughts.

The youth should be reprimanded for his familiarity with guests, and yet the chance to avoid the rest of the family beckoned like a lighthouse in a storm.

"No tea. If you could make it supper instead, I would appreciate it. And please tell the baron that I will plan to meet with him in the morning before I depart for home. I have been gone too long as it is."

"Very well, sir." After a quick bow, the footman scurried away and Grayson shut the door on his bride-to-be's outrage.

He would leave now except it would be quite late before he reached home and traveling alone on the dark roads was not safe. Not to mention he still needed to finalize the transfer of Phoebe's dowry before he left.

If that was the only benefit to this match, he would not leave without it. However, after their earlier interactions, he had little doubt that Lord Bainbridge would happily delay the delivery of the necessary funds just to remind Grayson of the disgusting offer he had refused.

A shudder coursed through his body at the thought of linking the Wentworth name to such a family. However, if the baron persisted in making things difficult, the lack of a dowry could be considered a breech of contract...

Grayson's lips twisted into the semblance of a smile. Only if he was willing to use the new penalty clause as a threat against the baron.

Either way, at least Danvers would get what they needed from the bargain.

As Grayson clenched his fist at the injustice, he belatedly recalled the strand of pearls in his hand.

In her current mood, Phoebe would likely destroy them.

He'd been equally disappointed in their engagement, but her childish temper tantrum did not bode well for a lifetime of marital harmony.

Wasn't there a passage in the Holy Scriptures about it being better to live with a dry morsel of bread in the corner of an attic than with a cantankerous woman?

Could he really bring her home to live in his castle by the sea? Would she help him rebuild the estate or tear it down around them within months?

Would he soon wish he had a mere cottage in the village instead? A cottage like Emma's?

Grayson pushed away the impossible thought and crossed the room once again to put his mother's necklace safely away. After all, the strand had been a treasured gift from his father upon Grayson's birth.

What would his father say about Phoebe? About the situation Grayson found himself in?

His childhood memories placed the stern man behind the solid desk in the library surrounded by stacks of papers and exerting a strong force of will. That man would have scolded his son for acting without thought and insisted he bear the consequences with dignity.

But on his deathbed, that same man had begged him to find a wife and win her heart. Despite the dusty letter forgotten in the corner of a drawer, his sire's wishes were for someone to make their manor a home again.

Someone like Emma. After all, his father had appreciated the years of service by Mrs. Richards enough to look after her family.

Perhaps Grayson could have honored the spirit of his promise by betrothing himself to Emma. He would have lost a dowry, but would have gained a different treasure.

Yet, without the betrothal letter as an introduction to the baron's household, would he have even spent enough time with Emma to see beyond their shared memories to her worth?

It was too late to know now.

Regret left him with a physical ache around his heart.

If only Emma were returning as mistress of the manor. She saw him as more than a walking title to advance her own status. She would have treasured a strand of pearls as a symbol of his love.

No. Grayson pushed aside the vision of her lovely face as he replaced the necklace into his bag beside the folded parchment.

He groaned. If only her name were on the document.

A document whose original terms had been altered by the resident baron without Grayson's approval.

Of their own accord, his eyes drifted to the writing desk with its quill and ink pot. It would be a simple enough task to replace the name of the bride. Or to alter the terms yet again.

On the corner of the desk sat a lantern with a striker. What if the contract accidentally caught on fire and was destroyed?

No.

Grayson rose and strode away from the temptation.

His integrity mattered and a Wentworth always kept his word. He needed to fear God, not man. Needed to do the right thing regardless of the cost. Had to respect himself before he could earn the respect of others.

He slammed a fist into the palm of his other hand. The contract would have to stand as written.

However...

Another truth filtered through his tangled emotions and took root. Self-respect also meant he could not honestly promise before God to love and honor Phoebe as his wife. That vow would defy both his personal feelings and the heart of his deathbed promise to his father.

God, I don't see any way out of this, but Wentworth Manor and Danvers need Emma even more than I do.

A sense of peace enveloped his heart.

Was it possible?

Yes. All he had to do was find the courage break the current contract and marry Emma instead. While somehow figuring out how to satisfy the vile penalty clause without losing his home.

Grayson paced the room in step with his cascading thoughts.

He could delay the current wedding plans until he had saved enough to pay the penalty. However, Lord Bainbridge would likely see through his excuses and calling off the wedding at a late date would damage Phoebe's reputation unnecessarily.

Would the baron accept a payment plan for the penalty or demand a lump sum? Could he borrow the money from somewhere else and then use Emma's inheritance as a down payment toward that loan? He wouldn't know for sure until he could talk to a banker in Launceston.

Except that solution would leave him and his bride with nothing until after the harvest...assuming Emma would still wish to marry him after breaking her heart.

Just an hour past, he'd heard the pain and betrayal in her voice as she learned of his engagement to her cousin. And that was before he had turned and seen her ashen face.

Yet, there had been a moment when her glistening eyes had swept over his face...a moment where it seemed she had recognized his emotions and felt sympathy for his plight.

But would it be enough?

Another knock on the door announced the arrival of his supper. With a nod, he accepted the silver tray from the servant, then after shutting the door, set the meal aside.

With a heart as hollow as the pit of his empty stomach, Grayson fell to his knees.

God, help me find a way out of this situation. Grant me wisdom.

After another restless night with little sleep—albeit for a different reason that the previous times—Emma found herself wide awake before dawn with a sense of urgency that she needed to leave her uncle's home while she had the chance.

She rolled to her side and glanced at the packed trunk near the foot of her bed with the single golden gown laid atop it. However, in order to make her escape, she would need to ask Mr. Stafford for help getting her belongings out of the house and to Mrs. Ashbrook's home.

Once in Whitstone, she could rent a carriage or wait for the public coach in order to get to Danvers. Except she didn't have any coins to pay her way, only a large bank draft.

Perhaps she could ask the cook or even the vicar for a temporary loan. After all, her inheritance documents proved she had the means of repayment.

She glanced at the window and the subtle lightening of the sky. It wouldn't be long before the household staff was about their tasks and hopefully she could be on her way before her uncle or cousin arose.

Phoebe's pouting rampage late yesterday afternoon had led to a stilted family dinner with a conspicuously absent guest. Her cousin had retired early while her uncle retreated to his study with a decanter of brandy.

Making it easy for Emma to finish her packing by candlelight, almost as if God had been watching over her and providing a way of escape.

A slamming door jolted Emma from her thoughts and she lurched upright as her uncle's deep voice bellowed down the hall.

What had happened?

After throwing back her covers, she snatched her wrapper from the foot of her bed and rushed out into the hall.

Two doors down, outside Phoebe's bedroom, the new upstairs maid, Louise, huddled against the wall with a hand over her mouth. At her feet sat an abandoned bucket of water as if she'd come to fill the wash stands and been interrupted. Or surprised.

From inside Phoebe's room came another voice, too deep for her to make out the words. A man's voice. Was it a physician?

Emma moved closer and quietly addressed the overwrought maid. "You can go. I'll see to the water myself."

The girl nodded, then scurried away.

"How dare you show your face around here?" Her uncle's voice trembled with rage.

"I invited him." Somehow her cousin managed to convey her irritation in the face of her father's anger.

Invited who? Emma stopped in the doorway and peeked inside.

"And how dare you accept his worthless promises? Did he tell you I refused him?"

In the light of a lamp beside the bed, Emma peeked beyond her uncle's velvet robed shoulder and spotted Phoebe propped upright against her pillows, clutching her bedding to her chest with her loose hair down around her bare shoulders.

Emma sucked in a quick breath. Since when did her cousin sleep without a bed gown?

"He did, but I don't care—"

"If you think I'll let you marry him now—"

"You're too late." The other male voice spoke again.

Emma's gaze swung to the far side of the bed where a partially clothed Mr. Smythe pulled on his shirt. She quickly looked down at her bare feet, clutching her wrapper tight around her waist.

Surely the man hadn't been...

May God have mercy and help them all.

"We're now married in word and deed." There was both glee and triumph in his tone.

Emma risked another glance. Mr. Smythe waved a folded parchment in the air, then winked at Phoebe.

Who giggled. Then blushed.

"Get out!" Her uncle's roar stopped Emma's heart for a beat and she stepped back into the hall.

Mr. Smythe nodded and picked up his boots. "Only long enough to fetch our witness. Then I'll be back to collect my wife."

The man brushed past Emma and boldly made his way toward the main stairs. As if he were a member of the family and had the right to be there.

"How could you disgrace yourself under my roof? You're no daughter of mine."

"Obviously, since you were about to force me to marry someone else." Phoebe lifted her chin. "I won't apologize for loving Francis."

"He's nothing." The baron waved a dismissive hand.

"He's my husband. The vicar married us yesterday."

Yesterday? The only time Phoebe had been away from home had been during their picnic...when she and Mr. Smythe had gone for a stroll near the bridge leading straight to the vicar's home.

As if the entire outing had been contrived as a convenient facade for their true purpose.

And Phoebe had forced her to be an unknowing part of the scheme.

Emma took another step backward and knocked over the bucket of water with a clatter.

"You." Her uncle rounded on her and skewered her with a glare. "You're *my* witness."

Emma swallowed hard, then forced the words out. "Witness? To what?" To her cousin's ruin? To the fact Mr. Smythe had apparently spent the night in her cousin's room?

"We'll get a special license and marry her off to Danvers today."

"What? No!" Phoebe's shriek of outrage was followed by a rustle of the covers as she catapulted out of the bed and grabbed for her dressing gown. "You can't. I'm already married."

"Easy enough to get an annulment, especially when Emma here tells the vicar she caught Danvers leaving your room." Her uncle stalked over and yanked the bell rope to summon a staff member.

Emma squared her shoulders. "No. I won't lie. The only person I saw leaving her room was Mr. Smythe." She waved a hand down the hall. "And Louise likely saw him here too."

Her uncle narrowed his eyes. "If she wishes to remain employed, she'll say that she saw him leaving *your* room."

"But that's impossible. I would never—"

"Then remember that your loyalty lies with your family and we'll leave that interloping swine out of this." The baron waved her away as if her feelings or reputation were of no value, then turned on his distraught daughter. "And you, thoughtless child, will get dressed immediately, but you will not set foot outside your door until I give you leave."

On shaking legs, Emma turned and ran back toward her room. At the end of the hall, the door to the servant's stairs opened and Mr. Stafford hurried forward in answer to the baron's summons.

Her uncle's plans for a cover-up would soon be set in motion.

Emma's knees trembled as she shut her door behind her. What madness had descended upon the household? As her uncle stated, did her loyalty truly lie with such a family?

Or to her mother's memory? To the stories she'd been told about her father? To her faith? To honor? To the truth?

She swallowed hard. It would dishonor all of the above to be a part of this deception and doom Lord Danvers—Grayson—to a marriage under such circumstances. Her childhood hero deserved much more.

Emma rushed to get dressed.

No matter the personal cost, she would at least give him the truth as a defense. Then there would be nothing her uncle could do.

However, knowing her uncle, he'd go to extreme lengths to force his will. In fact, if given the chance, he would love nothing more than to use her cottage, inheritance, and banknote as blackmailing leverage to force her to speak his lies or at the least remain silent.

She wouldn't give him the chance.

After tucking her precious documents and the banknote into the concealed pocket of her skirt for safekeeping, she added her bedclothes to her trunk.

Thanks to Phoebe's actions and her uncle's threat, it was even more important to make a speedy escape.

But not until she got a message to Grayson.

On quiet feet, she eased out into the empty corridor and headed toward the east wing. Except even from the main landing, she spotted her uncle's coachman, Percy, stationed outside one of the rooms.

The same man who had driven them on yesterday's picnic. Making his presence in the house further evidence of his role as her uncle's spy.

Her stomach cramped. If he thought it necessary, her uncle wouldn't think twice about locking her in her room as well.

As much as she'd love to storm down the hall, she was a woman, not a rescuing knight on horseback. And as such, she would need to come up with a different strategy to deliver her message.

Perhaps she could slip a note onto his breakfast tray, but she wouldn't put it past her uncle's servant to search the tray and confiscate the incriminating message.

Unless her message was hidden.

Emma turned toward the kitchen instead. There was more than one way to breach the defenses of Grayson's prison.

Chapter Eleven

A loud booming crash startled Grayson awake and he lifted his head from the pillows to cast bleary eyes in the direction of the noise.

The door to his room had been thrown open and Lord Bainbridge stood in the opening, dressed in black with hands propped on his hips and a scowl upon his face. "I would have a word with you."

"Now?" Grayson blinked. What time was it anyhow? Dim light filtered in around the drawn curtains but after praying until the wee hours of the morning, his sense of time was disoriented at best.

"Yes, now." Sarcasm laced the baron's tone as he strode into the room.

With a sigh, Grayson sat up and reached for his bed jacket. Obviously the man wasn't going to extend him the courtesy of dressing first.

"I had my reservations about betrothing you to my daughter, but believed you to be a man of honor like your father." Lord Bainbridge paced the carpets, glancing around as if searching for something.

"I am—"

"Rubbish." Spittle flew from his mouth as his face reddened. "Instead you answer my offer of hospitality by anticipating your vows and bespoiling my daughter under my own roof."

"I...what?" Was this some sort of a strange dream? "It isn't possible."

Lord Bainbridge jabbed a stout finger in his direction. "There were witnesses. And therefore you'll be married under special license as soon as it can be arranged. Later today, if possible."

Ignoring his state of undress, Grayson leapt from the bed and slashed a hand through the air. "No. I had already decided not to marry your daughter."

The other man blinked as if surprised, then narrowed his eyes. "But now you will." With another glance around the room, the baron strode toward the open door. "And to keep you from sneaking off like a coward, I'm setting my man on your heels."

Beyond the man's retreating form, Grayson caught a glimpse of yesterday's coachman standing in the hall before the door to his room slammed shut and he heard the unmistakable sound of a key turning in the lock.

What had just happened? Was he truly a prisoner here? Surely it was a bad dream brought on by a lack of supper and hours spent handing his mountain of worries over to God.

Except as he turned back toward the bed, Grayson stubbed his toes on the leg of a chair and the pain brought him fully awake.

It wasn't a dream, but rather a living nightmare. To be forced into marriage to a woman he did not even like?

And why?

Memories of her father's words came rushing back. Anticipating his vows and bespoiling his daughter? Heat rushed to Grayson's face and he shuddered at the very thought of being intimate with Phoebe even after a wedding.

But where would Lord Bainbridge have gotten such a foul idea? His anger and demands for a speedy resolution could not be forced. Even if the man's visual search for something—the betrothal contract lying about perhaps—made the rest of his outraged mannerisms seem rehearsed, something must have happened overnight to warrant a hasty wedding.

And Phoebe or others were willing to lie as witnesses to force his hand.

Could he plead for justice and a fair hearing? Probably not. Because with the baron's network of local connections and his earlier willingness to distribute bribes, the man would have no trouble getting a special license...or a magistrate to rule against Grayson.

After making the decision to cancel the contract no matter the personal cost, he'd fallen asleep with the assurance God was going to work things out in his favor.

Which made this pressured rush to fulfill the terms feel like an arch enemy binding constricting chains about his chest.

Enemy. It was a battle after all.

Something large was going on within the walls of Bainbridge Manor and only God knew the truth. Only God could get Grayson and the village of Danvers out of the deceitful web they were trapped in.

He clenched his hands atop his head and tugged on his hair in frustration.

God, You know I am innocent. And You alone can get me out of this mess. What am I to do?

Grayson's eyes swept around the room. He was too high up to risk using the window to escape, but he couldn't shake the strong impression that he was to pack his things anyway. As if his time in Whitstone was done.

Yes. He needed to be prepared for anything.

With resolve, he rose and quickly dressed, then gathered his belongings atop the rumpled bedding alongside his bags.

A slight knock on the door was followed by the distinctive click of the key turning the lock. The door swung open, admitting the butler personally delivering a tray of food with the coachman visibly standing guard.

His stomach cramped. "I'm not hungry."

"Sure you are, my lord." The butler raised an eyebrow at the obvious packing, then turned. "Shall I just set this up by the fireplace?"

"I don't—"

A slight cough interrupted him. "You should reconsider. The kitchen prepared a special treat today."

Something in the man's tone caught his attention and he studied the tray. There beside the tea pot was a small plate containing a party pocket just like the ones Emma's mother used to make for him.

A mixture of nostalgia and love swirled through his veins. Only one person could have made the pastry, and surely she had her reasons to send it today.

Did it contain a message for him? Did the butler know?

Grayson studied the butler's face as he set to transferring dishes from the tray to the small table. "Perhaps I will break my fast after all."

"Very well, my lord." A slight smile and nod branded him as a participant in whatever scheme Emma had planned.

Grayson reached to break open the flaky breading, but the butler halted his hand, then with a subtle tilt of his head toward the hall as a reminder of the guard, the butler stepped back.

"Just ring me if there's anything else you need this morning."

Right. He needed to pretend normalcy for the sake of the eavesdropper. And yet what should one say when being imprisoned against their will for a crime they were innocent of?

The butler's gaze dipped with a slight wink as if he understood the dilemma. "I hear there's to be a wedding later. Should I send someone to see to your clothes?"

A wedding.

Grayson swallowed hard, then forced the words through tight lips. "That would be most helpful."

The man lowered his voice. "Although we hope the bride is a different one?"

Grayson matched his tone. "I pray it is so."

The butler straightened and stepped back. "Very well, my lord. I'll return later with water for your bath."

Ah. Another excuse for visitors to return and the door to be reopened. Frequently.

Once the butler left, Grayson waited for the sound of the key in the lock before reaching once again for Emma's treat. He cracked it open, then pulled a folded piece of parchment from the center dropping the flaky bread back onto the dish.

Would this message be the key to his freedom?

Tears misted his eyes as he unfolded the note and he blinked several times before reading the writing inside.

"You are too honorable to be treated this way. The truth is..."

"Lord Bainbridge instructed me to ensure that a wedding feast be prepared for this evening's meal." Mrs. Carey addressed the kitchen staff from her place near the servant's stairs, then shot a frown at Emma standing beside the ovens. "Miss Clarke, do you agree that there will be a need for cake?"

Emma smoothed sweaty palms on her skirts and lifted her chin. "In my opinion, there is always the need for some sort of dessert with a meal, no matter the occasion."

The housekeeper's eyes narrowed briefly as if she weighed Emma's words for any signs of rebellion, then she shifted her gaze to encompass the room. "Very well. Be about your tasks." With a swish of her heavily-starched skirts, the woman left down the long hall to the breakfast room.

Near the work tables, Mrs. Ashbrook assigned the kitchen maids specific duties, then tilted her head toward the outer door.

Emma nodded before slipping outside to the gardens where they could talk privately.

A minute later, the manor's cook joined her and began gathering vegetables into a basket hung over her arm. "What is this about a wedding?"

She shook her head and swallowed the lump in her throat. God alone knew how the events of the day would resolve themselves. All Emma could do was be obedient in the small things.

"My dear—"

"I hope to leave this morning. My trunk is already packed, but I'll need directions and a conveyance to your house in the village. If your offer still stands..."

"Of course." The cook cast a quick glance over her shoulder back at the house. "Just a moment." Leaving her basket on the ground at Emma's feet, she entered the kitchen once more but returned a minute later.

"I've sent Dexter to fetch your trunk while Mrs. Carey is occupied elsewhere."

"Thank you. And I promise not to impose upon your hospitality for long."

Mrs. Ashbrook brushed her words aside and reached once again for the basket. "I knew your father when he was a boy and it's my pleasure to be of service to his daughter."

Emma blinked at the discovery of another ally in the house. First Mr. Stafford, and now the cook. If she'd considered it sooner, she might have learned more stories of her father's youth, but it was too late.

She needed to leave before her uncle pulled her into his wicked schemes...or even before Phoebe's actions were spread around the village and tainted Emma's reputation by association.

Mrs. Ashbrook leaned close and lowered her voice. "Now, what was that all about with that special treat you were a'baking this morning when I arrived? And having Mr. Stafford play errand boy for you?"

"It was the only way I could think to get a private message to Grayson. Lord Danvers."

"A private message?"

The woman's raised eyebrow too closely resembled her late mother's inquisitive stare and Emma squirmed. Then relented with the truth. "The way servants know everything that goes on under this roof, you've already heard what happened this morning and how my uncle is trying to force a different wedding."

Mrs. Ashbrook nodded as a grim look of disgust flitted across her features.

Emma blew out a long breath. "I merely thought he also deserved to know the truth so he can make the right choice."

"The right choice?"

"For him. And for Danvers."

"And for you?" The inquisitive eyebrow rose again pulling the truth from the depths of Emma's heart.

Heat rushed to her face. "There had been that possibility yesterday." Even if it was too much to hope that today would be different.

Her surrogate mother lowered her voice. "Do you love him?"

"Yes." That much was true. She sighed. "But it doesn't matter. After this, he'll want nothing to do with any of us. And even if he still wished to marry me, I would permanently lose the only family I have left."

Although she had survived the first seventeen years of her life without them.

"Since when have they treated you like family?" The woman grunted as she yanked several carrots from the earth, then propped a hand on her ample hip. "If you ask me, you should go build your own family with a man who will treat you like the treasure you are."

A man like Grayson.

Was it possible? Perhaps.

Something like hope blossomed within her chest. God had already gifted her with a home and income, so what other miracles might He perform?

Once she was settled back in Danvers, perhaps in time Grayson might forget about her cousin's behavior and her uncle's accusations. Might eventually remember their tentative connection.

Assuming he too was able to escape the walls of the manor. Could she truly leave the area without knowing his fate?

"Miss Emma?" Mr. Stafford's voice cut into her musings as he approached on the garden path. "Your presence is requested inside."

Her heart stopped for a moment, then raced with a furious beat. Should she make a dash for the village instead?

"Who wishes to see her?" Mrs. Ashbrook stepped between them.

The butler paused, then lowered his voice. "Lord Danvers is awaiting Miss Emma in the kitchen storage room."

"How did he—"

Mr. Stafford smirked. "I sent Percy on an errand to fetch the baron's large bathing tub, then guided our mutual friend to the servant's stairs. Dexter brought your trunk down first, but my son is currently hauling buckets of hot water into a heavily guarded—empty—room."

The cook snorted and Emma grinned at the image of her uncle's spy stationed beside the door.

Even better, Grayson was no longer imprisoned even if he was not yet truly free. And despite her family's behavior, he was asking for her.

"If you'll excuse me, I have a sudden desire to inventory the herbs." Emma turned toward the manor.

"I think I've enough vegetables for now." Mrs. Ashbrook's voice held more-than-a-trace of laughter. "Mr. Stafford, will you carry this for me?"

The voices of her friends faded behind her as Emma entered the kitchen. Ignoring the curious glances of the servants, she crossed to the storage room. Her eyes quickly adjusted to the dim light offered by a single lantern and spotted Grayson seated on her trunk with two other bags at his feet.

As she nudged the door mostly closed behind her, he rose with a steady gleam in his eyes. Gone was the bleak and pained expression of yesterday afternoon in her uncle's study.

"My dear Emma." He stepped closer and clasped her elbows, his large hands—and words—warming both her skin and her heart. "I couldn't explain what happened yesterday in front of your uncle."

When her hopes had been raised...and then dashed. Not caring to relive her disappointment, she shook her head.

"Please." He gently squeezed her arms until she nodded. "I made my father one promise on his deathbed, but when sorting through his papers I found a betrothal agreement."

"And that's why you came?"

"One reason. And to deliver your inheritance." His beautiful eyes peered into hers. "But that first night, we only had opportunity to discuss the first matter." He sighed and regret flitted across his face. "Suffice it to say that these new developments aren't the first time your uncle has manipulated a situation or played false with me."

She grimaced. In only a week, Grayson had uncovered what took her months to discover of her uncle's character. "But your father wanted the union?" Perhaps her uncle hadn't always been so unscrupulous.

"His last words were for me to find a wife and win her heart. I tried to do that based on the agreement I found, but the more I spent time with you, the more I struggled." He released her and swiped a hand down his face. "And yesterday, I sought out the baron to withdraw my offer."

She folded her arms over her chest as the memory of her heartache returned. "But instead you signed the contract."

His eyes pleaded with her for understanding. "Thanks to your uncle's goading, I had *already* signed the contract the first day I was here. Then yesterday, when he pulled it out to sign it, I saw he had added additional terms without my consent. But with my signature on the document, my integrity was at stake. Of course, he offered me a way out if I helped with the local smuggling operations."

She gasped. "You didn't—"

"I couldn't accept, which is why I ended up betrothed instead." He grasped her hands. "I made the best decision I could in the moment, but after much prayer last night, I realized I couldn't go through with the marriage even if he enacted the penalty clause."

"A penalty?" She blinked. She'd never heard of such a thing.

"It was his unsavory addition, but no matter the cost, I have to be true to myself." His lips curled into a slight smile as he echoed her words back.

No matter the cost. But he'd already told her how his father's illness had drained their funds.

She tugged her hand loose and fumbled for the opening in her skirts to reach her pocket. "I know it's not enough, but please take—"

"No." With a firm grip, he stopped her movements, then reached instead into his own jacket pocket and pulled out her note. "You've already given me exactly what I need."

"Truly?"

"But I must know..." Wrinkles appeared on his brow. "I saw how upset you were yesterday. I broke my word and I wouldn't blame you if you never forgave me, but why did you tell me this?"

Didn't he know? Couldn't he guess without her having to say it? However, she too had to be true to herself. "Because you deserve better."

Disappointment dimmed the earlier gleam in his eyes.

She swallowed her pride and whispered the rest of the truth. "Because I love you."

After a quick exhale, he pulled her into his arms, crushing her against his solid chest. "Oh, how I love you."

Her heart soared at the fervency of his declaration. Their future was still unclear, but somehow they would face it together.

Somehow.

Chapter Twelve

Grayson savored the sensation of Emma's slim curves in his arms and the warmth of her words around his heart. To love and to be loved. There was no greater feeling in the world and he would gladly spend his lifetime making her happy.

But first, he had to extricate himself from the current debacle so he was free to ask for her hand and make her his wife.

He sighed, then gave her one last squeeze before easing back and gazing down into her shining green eyes. "Thank you for loving me though I don't deserve it."

"I'm the one who isn't deserving." Her cheeks pinkened. "But now what? How much will you have to pay to be free of the contract?"

"Nothing." He lifted the crumpled note still in his hand. "With this, you've saved me from a disastrous marriage I didn't want."

Her smile faded. "How is that possible? I only wrote that I saw her with Mr. Smythe in a compromising situation and that he claimed they were married."

Grayson was tempted to kiss away the delightful wrinkle between her eyes, but there was time enough for affection later. At present, he needed distance in order to think like his lawyer classmates.

Should he start his arguments with the compromising situation or the marriage claim?

He turned on his heel and walked away. Three steps later, he'd reached the wall of shelves and had to turn back. "Is she truly married? And if so, when?"

Near the somewhat-open door, Emma nodded. "She said it was yesterday. I can only imagine it must have happened during our picnic when they disappeared on their walk. We were so busy talking that I'm not completely sure how long they were gone."

And in their absence, Grayson had finally recognized Emma's true identity. After which he'd been so distracted trying to hide his own feelings that only now did he recall the other couples' smiles when they had returned.

If they indeed were wed over the noon hour, that ceremony would have preceded the time on the contract in his pocket.

He made another lap around the small room. "Is there any proof of a wedding other than her word?"

"I saw Mr. Smythe waving a folded piece of parchment around." Emma's voice choked off into a whisper. "He said something about being married in word and deed."

The existence of a document implied a ceremony with witnesses, but it might be overturned or annulled unless...

"Did they..." How did one discover if the couple had consummated their vows? His face heated at the thought.

Obviously she caught his meaning for her face turned a vivid shade of red before she stared down at the stone floor. "Both were unclothed and um..."

"You saw this?" His jaw dropped. That was certainly a compromising situation if he'd ever heard of one.

She twisted her hands at her waist. "I heard yelling this morning before dawn. My uncle had arrived there first. I only saw her huddled under the covers and him half-dressed in the corner."

Grayson resumed his limited pacing as the arguments built. "Her compromised virtue could be grounds enough to break a betrothal, but marriage to another nullifies it completely." And if the Clarke family broke the contract, Grayson could be entitled to the dreaded penalty clause in reverse. If he wished to strike back and seek revenge for the way he'd been treated.

"But what if my uncle pursues an annulment? That's what he was threatening this morning." Emma's voice gained strength along with a hint of disgust. "Right before he demanded I tell the vicar that I had seen you in her room and that Mr. Smythe had been my visitor."

"None of which is true."

"I know. And I would never say it. Except he could lock me in my room like he did to you. He could even pressure the vicar by withholding his financial support and get the new upstairs maid to—"

"Don't worry. I highly doubt Mr. Smythe would ever agree with that story and from what I hear, his family holds a lot of influence in this region."

A small smile bent her lips. "True."

"However, even if they aren't married, the scene you observed is enough to break the contract." He came to a stop in front of her. "You are my witness. And you are my future."

Light sparked in her eyes and he covered her sigh with his lips. One kiss of promise turned into another, until he reluctantly pulled back.

Except he had to know.

"Once I am free, will you marry me?"

"Yes." She breathed the word and pressed a hand over her mother's locket at her neck.

A neck that should grace other jewelry. Jewelry from him. He quickly crossed to his bags and returned with the strand of pearls.

"Will you hold onto these as a symbol of my honest intentions? They belonged to my mother."

His Emma gasped in surprise, then nodded. "Fasten them for me?"

She turned slightly, and with trembling fingers, he somehow managed to drape the strand around her neck and secure the clasp.

"Other than my recent inheritance from your father, I don't have anything else to bring."

"You bring your heart and that is all I truly want." And somehow they would have to trust God for it to be enough.

A distinct cough outside the door gave them a moment's warning before the butler nudged the door fully open.

"Miss Emma, don't forget about your dowry."

"I don't have—"

"It was a bequest from your grandfather."

"What?" Her voice and body shook. "Are you sure? Because my uncle said—"

The meddling servant stepped into the room with a frown on his face. "He lies."

Emma lurched back and Grayson steadied her.

"I was a witness to your grandfather's joy when you were born and later a witness to the signing of his will. In memory of his son, he designated a gift upon your marriage and called you by name."

Emma gasped. "But he must have changed his mind later, because—"

"No. It was the last will. I know because there was also a bequest to my family in the terms."

"Perhaps my uncle didn't know?" Emma's voice quivered.

The butler shook his head. "He was the other witness at the signing."

As Emma's surprise over her unknown inheritance turned into a moan of betrayal, Grayson's mind spun with conflicting emotions.

Part of him wanted to storm into the baron's study and shake the man senseless for stealing from and lying to his own niece. And while the man had likely already destroyed the evidence of his father's will and spent her funds, a dowry would indeed be an unexpected God-sent blessing to tide them over until the harvest.

Emma swiveled to face him. "If my uncle decided to cause trouble for you, would my dowry cover the penalty in the contract?"

He squeezed her waist. "It would be more than enough, but I don't believe we need to worry about that."

"Alright. So what shall we do now?" Emma peered up at him, the trust in her eyes causing his chest to swell.

To be her hero was a challenge he'd willingly accept.

"We start by meeting with your uncle to resolve this nonsense regarding my betrothal to your married cousin." Grayson glanced over her shoulder at the hovering butler. "Then, we raise the subject of your dowry, with the help of our witness here."

The butler raised one eyebrow, then nodded.

Emma spun back to face the servant. "Mr. Stafford? You won't get into trouble for helping us, will you?" She glanced back over her shoulder at Grayson as if asking him a question. "I'm sure we can find a position..."

Ah. She must be worried about their finances and not want to make a promise he wouldn't or couldn't keep. But between his desire to make her happy and the fact his current staff was already at a minimum, the answer to her unspoken question was simple.

He nodded. "Provided all goes as expected, I don't see any reason why not. Faithfulness should be rewarded wherever it is found."

Mr. Stafford gave a slight bow. "Thank you, but I do still have my son to look after."

Grayson smiled at the subtle but diplomatic negotiation. "I can make a place for him as well."

The touch of a smile curved the man's lips. "I have always longed to spend time by the sea."

"I happen to know of a small cottage in Danvers..." Emma's soft voice suggested another ideal reward for the man who had already done so much to help them that day.

Grayson rested his hands on Emma's waist. Her compassion and generosity would serve her well as his baroness. His smile grew as he addressed the servant. "You can stay at Wentworth Manor once you arrive, but if you desire it after we are married, we will see you and your son comfortably settled in the village."

The man bowed. "I thank you, my lord, and gratefully accept your offer."

"Will you need traveling expenses?" It wasn't much, but Grayson had a few coins in his pocket.

His new servant dismissed the offer with a quick shake of his head. "I have enough set aside." The man turned his attention to Emma. "I would have left before now but wanted to keep an eye on you. It was what your grandfather would have wanted and as I told you before, I always admired your father when we were younger."

A quick hug from Emma made the butler stiffen and Grayson wrestle with a wave of jealousy.

The butler stepped back and cleared his throat as if awaiting instructions.

Right. There was still much to be done before they could be on their way. "With Mr. Stafford's help, we'll soon have this nasty business taken care of."

At the reminder of the upcoming confrontation, Emma sagged against him and Grayson wrapped an arm around her slender waist in support. "And then we leave for good. I've got my horse, but I'm not sure how we'll manage—"

Mr. Stafford coughed as if to cover a laugh, then proceeded to anticipate their needs. "I'll order a carriage brought round to deliver you to the village and have your baggage loaded for a quick departure."

Grayson raised an eyebrow. "Anything else?"

"Perhaps a luncheon to consume during your travels? I'll be standing by whenever you're ready." The butler dipped his head in a slight bow, then retreated from the room already issuing orders to others who had apparently been eavesdropping outside the room.

Emma giggled. "What would we do without him?"

"What indeed?" Grayson's dry tone made her laugh again.

"However, once we're safely away to the village, Mrs. Pembroke once told me we could rent a carriage there. With good roads, we should be in Danvers by evening." Bless the woman's meddling ways to provide him with a solution of his own. "However, we should probably make a brief stop by the vicar's house ourselves."

"Why?" Emma's breath caught and her eyes widened.

"Mostly to establish his cooperation and commitment to the truth." Another possibility presented itself and he tossed it into the discussion to see what Emma thought. "Not to mention, his wife seemed to like me. We could give her a choice piece of local gossip by having her witness our vows."

"Without reading the banns?" Emma's eyes widened as if she were overwhelmed at how fast her life was changing. "And is that even possible since I'm not of age and would need my guardian's permission?" She gasped as if just now realizing that was exactly what her cousin had already done.

Grayson caught the mixture of longing and fear in her eyes, but there was no reason to worry about that final complication since God had seen to all of the details. He answered her last comment first. "Your guardian won't be a hindrance to our marriage."

Her mouth opened in surprise and he gave into his attraction with another kiss.

After a minute, she pushed him away and raised starry eyes to his. "You have no idea how desperately I want to marry you..."

Grayson caught the hesitation in her voice. "But?" His heart stopped beating for a moment, but her smile melted his fears.

"I've always dreamed of getting married beside the sea."

The place where their story began.

The rightness of her suggestion wrapped around his heart. "And so we shall." He sealed his promise with a quick kiss. "In fact, we could invite the villagers and make this year's Midsummer's Eve celebration even better."

"That would be perfect." Emma's eyes shone and his heart soared in response.

As tempted as he was to stay in the storage room and savor their newfound connection, their future lay elsewhere. Grayson extended his elbow to her. "Shall we, my lady?"

With a wide smile, Emma rested her hand on his arm and they exited the room only to be delayed by a collective cheer of congratulations from the kitchen staff including a teary-eyed main cook who muttered something about a cake.

Obviously more of the staff than the butler adored her.

Emma broke away from his side long enough to embrace the woman and whisper something into her ear. Grayson bit back his smile at the suspicion that Wentworth Manor might soon employ yet another of her uncle's former staff.

No matter. He'd do anything to see her continue to smile.

However, he wasn't free yet.

"Emma?"

At his voice, she turned and then hurried back to his side. "You're right. Let's go see my uncle so we can get on with the rest of lives."

Chapter Thirteen

"What are you doing here?" Her uncle half-rose from behind his desk, then retook his seat. His narrowed gaze darted from Grayson to her and back again as a vein began to bulge on his forehead. "And where is the man I put at your door to guard you? Did she let you out?"

Emma stopped just inside the study, then caught her breath as the butler shut the door with a firm click. There would be no escape from her uncle's anger, but whatever happened next, at least they had a witness in the faithful servant.

She would have to trust God—and Grayson—for the outcome.

Please God, make a way for us.

"Never mind how I was set free, today is about the truth." Grayson strode forward. "I came inland to fulfill a promise while seeking a wife with frugality, honor, and integrity. There's only one under this roof that meets those criteria. And God saw fit to make her a precious memory from my childhood as well." He glanced back over his shoulder at Emma with a half-smile meant just for her. "I have asked your niece to marry me."

Her face heated with the memory of his kisses and her fingers drifted upward to skim across the pearls around her neck. Reality was so much better than a dream.

Her uncle practically growled as he stood. "That's impossible since we already have a contract. Give it to me now, because, at risk of bankrupting your estate, your signature binds you to my daughter—"

"You mean this contract?" Grayson's tone matched the serious expression on his face as he pulled a folded parchment from his jacket pocket and dangled it just out of her uncle's reach. "This worthless document will never stand up as enforceable in court for multiple reasons. First, your daughter's unseemly behavior in the wee hours of the morning is reason enough to void the contract. Second, there are the claims that she is already married to someone else which means the overnight activity in her bedchamber likely was a consummation of—"

"All lies!" Her uncle slapped a hand onto the wooden desktop. "And what is this blame on my daughter's behavior? You were the only man seen in the upper hall outside her room. I have a witness who saw you there." A glare sent her direction promised retribution if she did not immediately support his claim.

Instead, Emma stiffened her back. "No. I saw Mr. Smythe inside Phoebe's room and both were—"

"Traitor." Spittle flew from his mouth as he raged. "Where is your loyalty to the Clarke name?"

The name given to her by her father, but one she struggled to embrace if it meant supporting a falsehood and ruining the future of an innocent man. "I cannot believe my father would condone such lies."

Her uncle's lips curled in disgust as he shook his head. "He always did think he was too righteous for the rest of us. Seems you are indeed your father's daughter."

Something inside her chest burst to life at the confirmation her mother had married a man worthy to have been her husband, and along with a slight nudge from Mr. Stafford beside her, Emma found the courage to truly be herself.

She lifted her chin. "To answer your accusation, Lord Bainbridge, my loyalty is with the truth, my mother's memory..." Her eyes darted to Grayson standing nearby to lend his support. "And with my future husband."

At her declaration, a mixture of pride and love shone in his eyes. Just like earlier with a few of the staff in the kitchen, she felt treasured.

Grayson faced the baron. "Now, since it's clear that a member of *your* family broke the terms of the contract, it would seem that I am entitled to the penalty clause you so clearly inserted." He paused and her uncle's eyes widened.

That enormous penalty Grayson had been willing to pay in order to marry her would now come from her uncle instead?

But how was that possible? With two daughters currently in London shopping for their trousseaux, could he afford to pay? Assuming he was even willing to admit fault.

"If we cannot handle this as gentlemen, I'm sure a court would agree with me." Grayson paused long enough for her uncle to shift on his chair. "Especially when we call forth the witnesses to testify."

Her uncle's face paled. He certainly couldn't afford the scandal of a court appearance since the truth would tarnish his daughter's reputation even further...as well as that of her sisters. Emma's innocent cousins and their impending marriages.

It was too steep a price to pay. Surely Grayson wouldn't go that far?

"Although I don't believe we need to involve the authorities, do we?"

Her uncle swallowed hard and shrank back in his chair, before offering a slight shake of his head as if admitting defeat.

Grayson's posture relaxed. "However, you should be relieved that I know of a third reason this agreement is worthless. And it allows us both to exit this unfortunate contract in the easiest manner possible."

Her uncle leaned forward.

Emma held her breath. What other reason could there be?

"If I've done the math correctly, your daughter's vows were spoken *before* you signed this betrothal contract making it inherently invalid and unenforceable since your daughter was already married. You were so thorough as to add the time when you signed and I'm sure the vicar will confirm the time of the ceremony as occurring near noon. During the picnic Emma and I attended with the happy couple." He chuckled. "With this contract thereby voided, the penalty clause becomes equally invalid and there would be no reason to ever argue the case in court."

Emma found her smile at Grayson's wise maneuvering of the discussion. After rightly threatening both a heavy financial penalty and humiliating public trial, he'd swept both from the table in an act of mercy that left him with the upper hand in the negotiations.

"No contract, no penalty. No harm, no foul." Her uncle's voice held equal parts relief and wry admiration.

"And I'll leave today unentangled and free to marry whomever I wish." Grayson's voice rang with conviction as he stepped forward and picked up the quill from her uncle's desk. "Now, just in case you should decide to change your mind later and try to blackmail into cooperation with one of your other schemes, we'll make this official now. I'm voiding this contract, then you will sign first along with Mr. Stafford as an additional witness to this conversation." With a slashing motion, he wrote something across the entire page and handed the quill to her uncle.

A moment later, he dipped the tip in the ink and added his signature. The butler stepped forward and signed with a flourish, followed lastly by Grayson.

"Of course, I'll hold onto this as proof. Just in case any word of this unfortunate situation ever leaks out." A hint of steel in Grayson's voice as he pocketed the document made it clear he would stand for justice at all costs.

After a moment's hesitation, her uncle nodded, but this time his agreement came with a small glare instead of a posture of defeat.

Grayson shrugged his broad shoulders as if unaffected by her uncle's mood. "I wish you luck sorting things out with your new son-in-law and his family."

Emma blinked at the reminder. As livid as he'd been earlier at Phoebe's behavior or their unauthorized overnight guest, her uncle did not dare ostracize a relative of the Jamaica Inn crew, especially since Grayson would never cooperate with smuggling along the coast. The irony of her uncle's reversed position was not lost on her.

Grayson stepped back from the desk and gave a slight bow. "Now, if you'll excuse me, having won her heart, my future bride and I have a long way to travel today." He turned and met her near the door, extending his elbow.

She slipped her hand onto his arm, more than happy to escape. But weren't they forgetting something?

"No. You can't marry her." Across the room, her uncle sputtered. "I won't let you."

Grayson raised an eyebrow as he turned them to face the new obstacle to their happiness. "On what grounds?"

"I'm her uncle. She's a minor and therefore needs my permission to marry since I'm her guardian."

Emma's hand shook on her fiance's arm. "No. Since my stepfather's death, Lord Danvers has been my guardian."

"Perhaps the elder baron was before your mother died, but guardianship is not inherited." Her uncle sneered.

"But it can be appointed." Grayson's voice was as firm as the hand he rested atop her trembling fingers. "I have written orders from the Court of Chancery reaffirming all the wards under my father's supervision. And as her legal guardian, without a doubt, I certainly give my permission for Emma to marry."

The wink aimed her direction sent her smile blooming once again.

Behind them near the door, Mr. Stafford cleared his throat.

Grayson glanced over his shoulder with a quirked smile, then turned back to her uncle. "I had almost forgotten. As Emma's guardian, I also have legal charge over her property, including her dowry."

Ah. He hadn't forgotten but had instead been leading her uncle into another trap by getting him to acknowledge Grayson's role as legal guardian first. His wisdom would serve Danvers well in the future.

"Her dowry?" A scoffing laugh burst from behind the desk. "She has nothing."

Emma winced at the words he'd thrown in her face on multiple occasions.

Grayson shook his head. "It has come to my attention by a witness to the will, that the late Lord Bainbridge designated a dowry be set aside for the daughter of his second son."

Even if her grandfather was now as gone as her mother's sister, the reminder that she had been treasured by a few members of the Clarke family soothed her lonely heart.

Her uncle was not one of those few for he quickly stood, shaking his head. "I know of no such thing."

"That is hard to believe, my lord, since your signature is on the document as a witness." Mr. Stafford winked at Emma as he passed by, pulling a paper from his pocket. "Since he was also leaving my family a reward for our many years of faithful service, the late Lord Bainbridge gave me a copy for safekeeping before his death." The butler opened it and pointed to a spot, presumably the present baron's signature.

Her uncle glared at the butler. "There were so many documents at the end, I must have forgotten about this one." His eyes skimmed the parchment and then he pursed his lips as he named a significant amount. "The bequest did, in fact, include my niece."

It was true. She had a dowry. And beyond saving the estate one hundred pounds a year for her support, she now had a treasure to contribute to the future stability of her beloved Danvers.

Grayson's voice cut through the tension in the room. "Since we are leaving today and plan to marry during the festival, I respectfully request an immediate transfer of Miss Clarke's funds. That will then conclude *all* of our business."

She could almost see the thoughts tumbling behind her uncle's troubled eyes as he considered his response. But then, his frown eased.

He slid open his top drawer. "Unfortunately, I am short of coins, so surely a bank note will be—"

"No, m'lord." Mr. Stafford pivoted to face them.

Grayson's arm tensed beneath her hand. "Is there a problem?"

The butler cast a quick glance at his current employer before answering his future one. "He lies. I know that he keeps more than sufficient funds locked in the bottom drawer beneath a false compartment. Which makes one doubt the worth of his note."

"Traitor!" Her uncle's face was a vivid shade of purple again.

"Thank you once again for your integrity, Mr. Stafford." Grayson turned to her uncle with a slight smile. "If you don't mind, I'll watch as you count them out."

"Your position is immediately terminated." Her uncle glared at his servant.

"With pleasure." The butler offered a slightly mocking bow.

A bit of shock flashed across her uncle's face.

Grayson's cleared throat brought them back to the present. "Come now. We haven't all day to wait."

Her uncle grumbled something, then bent around his large belly to reach toward his feet. Soon she watched a pile of shining coins mound up on the polished wood.

Coins her uncle would have gladly kept hidden away even if it meant stealing from his niece.

Emma bit her lip to stop her tears at the memory of yesterday in this very room when the same man had argued that she never needed to know about her inheritance from the late Lord Danvers.

All while he'd been hiding the truth of a different inheritance for the past two years.

The proof of his dishonesty clinked on the desk before her and she would be happy to leave the man behind to wallow in his web of deceit.

While Grayson counted the coins into neat stacks, Mr. Stafford left the room for a few minutes, then returned with a leather satchel to transport the payment. Grayson nodded his appreciation and began transferring the coins.

Something she should have thought of, but then again she had never needed a reticule to carry even the smallest of amounts since she had no coin and all of her purchases in the village for the manor were put on the baron's account.

Would any of that change once she was Grayson's wife? Perhaps, but for now, she slipped a hand into her pocket and savored the feel of the bank note hidden there.

Grayson fastened the bag closed, then scribbled out a receipt for her uncle. "Mr. Stafford, before you leave, are you owed anything?"

A flash of surprise crossed the former butler's face followed by a hint of satisfaction. "Half a month's wages for both my son and I."

"And your family's inheritance?" Grayson pointed to his jacket where the late baron's will had been kept.

The loyal servant straightened his shoulders. "Three hundred pounds is still owed before I will destroy the promissory note."

Nearby her uncle growled and leaned down once again to retrieve more coins from their hiding place. A few minutes later, they left her defeated uncle in his study and made their way toward the main entry.

And her future.

With one hand on the baron's sleeve, his mother's pearls around her neck, and her dowry in his possession, Emma could not contain her smile as she stepped through the double doors.

At the foot of the stairs, an open carriage awaited with a dark horse tethered behind. From around the corner of the manor, Dexter approached carrying her trunk and Mr. Stafford quickly bypassed their descent on his way to help his son.

Before long, she was seated in the carriage while Grayson checked the baggage and hid her funds somewhere in their depths. While several of her friends among the staff gathered just out of sight of the main doors to wish her well, she risked a glance upward toward the west wing to find Phoebe watching their departure, framed in her bedroom window.

Emma lifted her hand in farewell, then offered a brief prayer for her cousin's future happiness despite the choices she had made.

A moment later, Grayson took his seat beside her in the carriage. "Are you ready, my love?"

"I am." Her eyes swept over his handsome profile, catching the twinkle in his gray-blue eyes an instant before he leaned down to stake his claim with a kiss.

A very public kiss that sparked a cheer from the gathered servants and a snap of the reins from Dexter, their driver, to send them on their way.

Joy bubbled up into laughter. "You are a rascal."

"And...?"

"And I love you." Captivated by the warmth in his eyes, she found it somewhat difficult to breathe. For despite the pain of her past, God had surely blessed her.

"You are truly a treasure, my Emma soon-to-be-Wentworth." Grayson's husky tone did nothing to calm her romantic notions.

Her smile grew even larger. "I like the sound of that."

"Good. Because so do I." With a wink, he settled beside her for the first leg of their journey. After a brief stop to change carriages, they would soon be on their way toward the sea...and home.

And their future.

Halfway to the village of Whitstone, she spotted another open carriage coming toward them and soon identified the occupants as a grim

Mr. Smythe and a resigned-looking Mr. Pembroke. The vicar raised his eyebrows once he apparently recognized them in return.

Should they stop? She darted a quick glance at Grayson.

A smile curved his lips as he linked their hands, then lifted them high for the vicar to see before kissing her again. This time, by the time his lips lifted, her heart was about to burst out of her chest with the depth of her love.

She could not contain her smile as the other carriage passed by. Nor ignore the kindly vicar's answering nod of approval.

"I think that settled things quite nicely, don't you think?" Grayson's shoulders shook with his laughter.

"You truly are a rascal." Hopefully their children would take after their father in all the ways that truly mattered.

"And you wouldn't have me any other way." With another wink, he tugged her closer to his side.

Life would never be dull in Danvers.

As fairy tales went, real life was better than she had ever imagined. The handsome prince of a man had rescued her from a life of servitude and was taking her home to his castle by the sea.

And better yet, the same boy who had captured her childhood affections and occupied her dreams had grown into the man who had won her heart.

You've finished this book, so what's next?

Want more castle stories?

Can true love survive the distance when the road back to happily-ever-after is littered with secrets, a scandal, and a shocking revelation? Journey to Yorkshire for this Regency twist on the secret baby trope.

Read on for a preview of the next book in the series: *The Lost Heir*

If you'd like to receive updates about upcoming books or sales, you can sign up for email list on my website at CandeeFick.com.

(There might be a few surprises headed your way including a free novella and other exclusive bonus content.)

Dear Reader,

Thank you for spending a few hours of your time with me.

There is no greater pleasure as an author than knowing that I've encouraged my readers! If you enjoyed this book, please take a few minutes to let the rest of the world know by leaving a review at your favorite retailer or on sites like Goodreads or BookBub. It doesn't have to be long. Just a few words pointing other readers this direction would be much appreciated.

As I continue to write stories of faith, hope, and love, my prayer is that you will experience the amazing love of God and find encouragement for the journey called life.

Until we (hopefully) meet again in the pages of a book, happy reading everyone!

Candee

Preview: The Lost Heir

Within the Castle Gates series, Book Three

In Regency England, news travels slowly. Especially in Yorkshire.

Overnight, Kathleen Harris, a foundling raised by a vicar and his wife, becomes the ward of the Earl of Wiltshire and is set on a direct path to a London season. Now miles from home, will her heart outgrow her small Yorkshire village and the love of her childhood friend?

Reuben Cooke, a quality weaver in a region where the woolen industry thrives, supports his widowed mother and hopes to marry soon. However, after the local vicar dies, his dreams of a quiet life with Kathleen at his side quickly unravel as they are ripped apart by societal conventions.

Can true love survive the distance when the road back to happily-ever-after is littered with secrets, a scandal, and a shocking revelation?

Prologue

Mid-March 1790, Belgrave Manor

Breaking her fast alone still took getting used to.

However, alone was a relative statement for the liveried footman standing at attention beside the breakfast room's ornate sideboard gave credit to her meticulous hostess, Lady Beaumont.

Mrs. Armstrong swallowed her sip of tea and returned her china cup to the saucer before picking at the usually tempting morsels on her plate. She forced herself to take a bite.

And then another.

She needed her strength for the days ahead.

Oh, if only her Ned were here then she could lean on him in this time of horrific loss.

She blinked away the sudden rush of tears.

How could it be true? Shouldn't her heart have sensed the trouble long before the news finally reached her last eve?

And yet a fortnight had passed since the fire at the coaching inn in Wheatley had left her an orphan, claiming the lives of her parents and siblings. Almost a fortnight since their mass funerals. And over a fortnight since she'd penned the letter to Ned in London announcing her change of plans.

Why he hadn't come or at least sent word? What business was keeping him away?

Pray heaven that his time in town among those of rank had not turned his head or filled him with regret over her simpler upbringing.

The sharp pain squeezing her chest spread to her enlarged midsection and she set down her fork in order to rest her hand atop the increasing evidence of their child.

With weeks to go before her confinement, she'd been the logical—albeit last minute—substitution to serve as companion during her aunt's convalescence after a fall.

But mending a broken bone was simpler than mending a broken heart. And what cruel irony to have escaped mere rumors of a spreading pestilence when the real danger had been an unswept chimney that doomed the inn's inhabitants to a fiery fate.

Leaving her with a widowed aunt and her precious Ned as family.

If only he was near to offer comfort and prayers on her behalf.

She would ask Lady Beaumont to send a messenger to his family's London home posthaste, but such a request must wait until they were settled over their embroidery in the drawing room.

After all, since her injuries, the lady of the house took a breakfast tray in her rooms and only admitted her lady's maid into her inner sanctum.

And today her hostess was equally burdened with her own grief.

"M'lady?"

She glanced up to see the butler near her elbow with a folded newspaper presented on a silver tray.

"Perhaps something to distract you from your woes?"

"Indeed." She swallowed hard and reached for the offering. "I thank you for your kindness."

Living amidst such luxury and exercising the required formalities had been an adjustment, but her mother's sister had married well and after her husband's untimely death, Lady Beaumont was left a proper estate complete with a household of servants and an annual income. And as the lady's niece, the inevitable lessons in proper decorum would serve her well in the future. Ned would surely be pleased at the change.

She unfolded the paper and began to read while sipping on a fresh cup of tea. The first reports were from the House of Lords followed by the

House of Commons and by the time she'd finished her tea, she'd turned the page to such items as a salary for the speaker and the consideration of a large bounty for surgeons on slave ships if they provided proof that no more than two slaves in each hundred taken onboard perished.

Her stomach revolted at such a situation and she moved to the next report of mutiny onboard the HMS Bounty. How could God fearing sailors not only defy their authority but set them adrift with meager provisions to fend for themselves against the tides and the natives?

Another harsh cramp beset her and she breathed slowly through the pain that had spread to her lower back.

Already burdened by her grief, the heavy news of the world was too much to bear. Perhaps a lighter distraction?

As the tension eased, her eyes skimmed the page, falling upon the notice of an estate being sold at auction. A reward being offered for the return of a lost greyhound. And an employment posting seeking shoemakers.

Yes. The mundane aspects of life.

She smiled and turned the page yet again, eventually locating the marriage announcements and other items of society gossip. Her aunt would enjoy dissecting the matrimonial news over their stitching.

Midway down the first column was the news that the banns had been read for the Earl of Wiltshire.

Her eyes widened. A man on his deathbed made for an unusual groom.

A whisper escaped her lips as she read on. A small private ceremony was planned in deference to the recent tragedies in the family. The bride was previously betrothed to the Viscount Lewisham.

She held her breath. The viscount's death in a hunting accident a month ago was the reason Ned had left her side in the first place.

The announcement continued. In addition to grieving the loss of his father and two elder brothers, the Sixth Earl had recently lost his first wife in a fire...

"No!" She pushed back her chair and jumped to her feet. "It cannot be."

The footman rushed to her side. "M'lady?"

A vicious pain sliced across her abdomen and she clutched the edge of the table as a flood of warm liquid washed over her feet.

Tears burned her eyes and she panted for breath. "Dear God. It's too soon for the babe..."

Get the rest of The Lost Heir today.

More Fiction

A complete and up-to-date list of all my books can be found on my website at CandeeFick.com

Standalone Romance

Catch of a Lifetime (Cassie and Reed)

The Wardrobe Series

(Contemporary romance in theater settings)
Dance Over Me (Dani and Alex)
Focus on Love (Liz and Ryan)

Sing a New Song (Gloria and Nick)
A Picture Perfect Christmas (Liz and Ryan continued)
Home For Christmas (Grace and Tyler)
Complete Series Boxed Set

Within the Castle Gates Series

(Historical romance in various time periods)
Stepping Into the Light (Moira and Evan)
To Win Her Heart (Emma and Grayson)
The Lost Heir (Kathleen and Reuben)
Finding Home (Susannah and Nicholas)
Saving Grace (contemporary - Grace and Drew)
A Castle in the Clouds (Miranda and Josh)
Books 1-4 Boxed Set

About Candee

Candee Fick is a multipublished, award-winning author. She is also the wife of a high school football coach and the mother of three children, including a daughter with a rare genetic syndrome. When not busy writing, editing, or coaching other authors, she can be found exploring the great Colorado outdoors, indulging in dark chocolate, and savoring happily-ever-after endings through a good book.

Visit her website at CandeeFick.com where you can find out about her latest releases and sign up for her email list.

www.ingramcontent.com/pod-product-compliance
Lightning Source LLC
Chambersburg PA
CBHW022022170626
46808CB00003B/1025